WILD PALOMINO

STEPHEN HOLT

Wild Palomino

STALLION OF THE PRAIRIES

ILLUSTRATED BY

W. C. NIMS

GROSSET & DUNLAP

Publishers, New York

By arrangement with Longmans, Green and Co., Inc.

Printed in the United States of America

To My Son

HARLAN

CONTENTS

CONTENTS

CHAPTER I

TROUBLE

DES HARMON CAME INTO THE SHABBY LIVING ROOM of *Twin Anchor Ranch* and slumped down on the old horsehair sofa. A braided rawhide lariat sprawled up his hard brown arm, and fifty odd handbills tried to escape his right hand. The bills were pink and blue and white. And they said in heavy accusing black ink, BANK-RUPT SALE. Below, in finer print, they told about the breeding and excellence of the Palomino mares and colts to be sold.

Des reached a booted foot to drag a pine table closer, then flung the handbills on it, watching them cascade to the braided rag rug under the table.

"Whammo!" he said, ruefully eyeing the bills. "There goes the ranch, Saturday. I've nailed up a million of these on every crossroads fence post in Alberta." He flopped back and stared at the ceiling. "I guess when Dad gets back from the South Pacific he'll be plenty disgusted with the kids he left to run things."

Swallowing hard, Des fumbled inside his leather jacket and pulled out a letter from Lynn MacLean at Broken Arrow, two hundred miles to the north and west of *Twin Anchor*. Ripping it open, he began to read. First in moody silence, then exclaiming, and with eyes racing along the lines.

"Boy!" he breathed. "Boy, oh, boy!"

Harry, Des' blond twin brother came in from the kitchen.

"Well," he demanded, eyeing Des' face. "What's going on?"

Des went on reading. All the slack was out of his slim body now, and there was sparkle in his eyes.

Harry dived for him.

Des, from long practice, leaped clear, then flung the letter for Harry to pick up.

"Rocket's back again," he said, softly. "You know, that phantom colt that showed up last summer on Soda Springs Flats, and then disappeared."

Harry read the first page of the letter, then gave a low whistle.

"What do you know," he breathed. "Back again! That wild Palomino stallion!"

Des nodded.

"That's what Lynn MacLean says right there in the letter. The colt must have drifted in from the Blood Indian reservation herding a bunch of cayuse mares. Couldn't stand the noise from Lethbridge bombing range, I guess."

Harry agreed with a shake of his blond head.

"I'll bet he's a sight for sore eyes—all gold and silver," he whispered.

"Yeah, and as fast as chain lightning." Des let his eyes go thoughtfully out of the north window, where Estrellita, a young Palomino mare they'd intended breaking to saddle, stood nickering. Then off to the left of her, where twenty golden Palomino mares grazed and kicked in the June sunshine.

"Hey!" Des caught his breath and looked at Harry. An idea began to take shape in his mind.

Harry looked puzzled.

Des walked over to the window and, releasing the lock in the middle, raised the lower half.

The smell of green alfalfa from the meadow filled his nose. The old red barn with the back end burned off caught his eyes. That was where Hector, their Palomino sire had been burned to death, losing the *Twin Anchor* a whole season of colts. There'd been no money to buy another stallion.

Des stuck his head out the window, and breathed deep, and suddenly the answer came to him.

"You know, Harry," he said, pulling in his head and facing his twin. "That phantom stallion's our answer. The sire we need around here."

Harry caught on.

"We'd show Dad some colts that'd knock his eye out," he exclaimed.

"And Hawkins down at the bank, too." Des nodded. "If he'd put off this sale that's coming up Saturday."

"And this is Wednesday, I'd forgot," Harry groaned.

Before they could more than stare at one another, Janet, their young sister, came flouncing in. A yellow pup dressed in a pink doll dress and baby bonnet squirmed under her skinny brown arm.

"Boy's crazy," she said gravely, talking to her pup. "That colt's only been seen twice, Lynn told me last summer. An' he's smarter'n most people. Lynn said that, too."

Des' and Harry's eyes met in disgust.

But Janet went right on talking to her pup. "And if they did catch him on Soda Springs Flats, which is fifty miles long, I suppose they'd ride him home like a plow horse." She sniffed and turned the pup upside down against her flat chest. "Across the bombing range, fording rivers, and everything."

"It's not so much," Des said.

Mom, little and dark, like Des, came in just then, her fingers flying over knitting needles on a sock for Dad. A smile, that no amount of worry and hardship had ever been able to erase, lurked at the corners of her small firm mouth.

"What's not so much, Des?" she asked, softly.

"Des' crazy scheme. Ow! Help!" Janet dived behind her mother's calico skirt and peeked defiantly around it at the boys.

But the secret was out.

"Well?" Mom asked, waiting.

When they told her, she looked silently from one to the other, a soft flush mounting her cheeks. Then, still not speaking, she turned and walked to the window Des had raised. Pulling back the white curtain, she looked west across the horizon.

Des watched her trembling lips. Dad was out there on a destroyer, a lieutenant. And surely the war was nearly over. Maybe it was over by now. But you just couldn't get out of the Navy by snapping your fingers. There'd be years of patrol duty, watching the Japanese.

"Mom," he urged, "it's our only chance to dodge this dispersal sale. To lift this ranch up on its feet."

"Sure," blurted Harry. "What kind of sons are we to let Dad go to war and let this ranch go blooey? What kind am I, I mean—for I'm going." He faced Des squarely. "I'm twenty minutes older and an inch taller."

Des studied a moment. It was a way he had. At length, he said, "Lynn wrote me."

"I'm just as much his friend," Harry retorted. "And I'm going."

"Boys! Boys!" Mrs. Harmon raised her eyes to them. "I haven't said either of you could go yet."

"It's a cinch," Janet whispered loudly to her pup.

"Well—I declare, that child." Mrs. Harmon sank into a rocker, staring at Janet.

Des and Harry froze, waiting for her to speak.

And suddenly, Mom smiled. That same smile she'd worn when Jim Harmon had come in from the barn and announced, "It's no use, Sylvia. I've got to go. Every man is needed."

She said now, softly to Des and Harry, "But, are you sure? It's so dangerous—a wild Palomino?"

"Of course I'm sure," Harry exclaimed. "I'm grown up."

Mom smiled, and knit five stitches before Des spoke.

"Mom, it's this way," he said, thoughtfully. "I've been riding since I was born. And, I've taken that course in horse taming—the University of Alberta course."

Harry snorted.

Des flushed.

"Okay, laugh—but you'll see."

Then Mom smiled. "One of you may go."

"What about the sale?" piped Janet.

Mom's lips set. "There will be no sale for"—her eyes sought Des' in panic when she thought of Hawkins the banker—"a month?" she whispered.

Harry whooped. "That's time enough. And, I'm go-ing."

Des stood shaking his head, his lips a set line.

There was no sound in the tense room.

Suddenly from the meadow came the high-spirited nicker of Estrellita.

Des' and Harry's eyes met.

"Catch her!" Harry exclaimed. "It's what we'll be up against with Rocket."

"And the one that does the best job in the quickest time goes," Des added softly.

They surged toward the door, with Janet lugging her pup in hot pursuit. "I'll be judge and timekeeper. Give me your watch, Des," she puffed, catching up.

They moved toward a little grassy knoll overlooking the meadow, Des unstrapping the wrist watch his Dad had given him and putting it on Janet's arm as they walked.

"Okay," he said, then turned to Harry, at the knoll.

A tense silence fell between them.

"Well," Harry finally asked, "who makes first try? And I'd just as soon skip first chance."

"Draw straws," piped Janet. Stooping down, she picked a clover stalk and, turning her back for a second, swung to hold out a slim hand. "Short straw tries first," she shrilled.

Harry took hold of a bit of stem and drew out a piece
he could scarcely hold on to.

"Okay," he shrugged, then taking a deep breath and,
with only a glance at Janet, ran pell-mell for the barn,
got his saddle horse—a lean gelding—and raced toward
Estrellita.

The mare raised her head as Harry rode swiftly down
on her. Then, with almost a grin on her blaze face, she
darted into the herd of mares.

Harry sped through the sedate mares in pursuit. He
rode top speed till the sweat stood out on his pony's
neck.

Estrellita, fresh, and with silver tail over her arched
back, matched him stride for stride. She ran along the
creek, under the willows, splashing water up her golden
legs.

Harry's face was red. He leaned forward in the saddle
and shouted, pursuing her.

The mares grew excited and started running across the
flat green meadow.

Harry followed.

Estrellita broke from the herd and ran clean around
the buildings and corral, swerved toward the barn,
changed her fickle mind and ran back to the herd.

Harry, on his horse, grimly followed.

"Stay with her," encouraged Janet, shrilly. "You'll

run her down. And you've only been fifteen minutes—"

Harry waved and raced after the flying mare.

At length he cut her out from the herd.

"Now watch!" he yelled, setting his horse after her. His horse was well trained; he darted and followed every move of the mare, his long neck trailing her every move.

She tried to cut to the right.

Harry's horse cut her off.

"Yipee!" Harry yelled, swinging his quirt.

Estrellita swung to the left.

The saddle horse headed her.

And just ahead yawned the corral with the big plank gate opened wide.

Des gulped as he watched. But an admiring grin covered his face. Harry was doing a good job, and in less than twenty minutes. He began to move down toward the corral, his rope dangling on his arm.

In a second, Harry would have Estrellita in the corral and his rope on her.

Even as he looked up, Estrellita swept through the gate and into the corral.

Harry, racing toward the gate, shouted, "I've got you, girl!" Then let his voice trail off.

Des looked up just in time to see the mare skim the width of the corral, gather herself in a lithe knot of golden muscle and sail into the air.

A second later, she landed gracefully on the outside, and with a disdainful snort raced for the herd. Free.

Harry stood disconsolately by the half-shut gate as Des came up.

"Tough," Des said.

Harry's face presented a struggle, then broke into a sporting grin. "Some jump," he said, handing Des the reins to his saddle horse. "Let's see what luck you have?"

"Eighteen minutes' worth, Harry," Janet piped, puffing toward the boys.

Des stood watching the flying mare as she reached the herd and dropped her head to graze. He remembered parts of a book he'd read on horse taming.

Suddenly, he handed the reins back to Harry. His heart began to pound.

"Guess I'll try a new wrinkle," he said, softly.

"One minute gone," Janet warned.

Des grinned at her, then uncoiling his rope, walked rapidly down along the slope, across it, and within fifty feet of Estrellita.

"Come on, old girl," he breathed. "I'm not going to hurt you."

"No, nor catch me either," Estrellita seemed to say. Lifting her tail over her satin back, she trotted a dozen stiff-legged paces, then stopped and snorted again.

Des whistled a low soft tantalizing tune.

He made a loop in his lariat and swinging it in a small arc moved toward her, still whistling.

Estrellita forgot to graze. She followed the coiled loop with her soft brown eyes, her pointed ears cocked forward, listening.

Des moved closer, his throat dry, but being careful to make no false moves.

The mare edged away.

Des stopped. From the corner of his eye, he could see Janet studying the watch on her arm.

Estrellita stopped.

Des moved again, keeping up that soft coaxing whistle.

Estrellita moved. Then stopped, her soft ears flicking forward, then back.

"Ten minutes gone," Janet called from the knoll.

"Hush!" Harry, beside her, warned.

Des gulped. Eight minutes to go. Of course he could have longer, but if he got Estrellita under that time it would be fair to call it a win—Harry wouldn't ask for another try.

Softly, he put one foot in front of the other, keeping up his whistling, being careful to swing the loop, monotonously, steadily.

Estrellita stood transfixed, her soft brown eyes on Des, her pink nostrils dilating.

Des moved to within ten feet of her.

Estrellita began to tremble.

Des stopped whistling and spoke softly, letting his lariat move slower and slower.

He came within two feet.

He started to put out his hand.

Suddenly, from the distance, came the sharp crack of the corral gate banging shut against the pole fastener.

It broke the spell, Des realized.

Estrellita leaped clear, turned, and started away.

For a wild instant, Des hesitated. He'd lost. And he had been winning fairly. Then, acting from reflex, his hand moved with lightning rapidity. The soft grass would break her fall. With one co-ordinated motion, he sent the soft loop of his lariat in a swirling motion. The rope feeding from the loops in his left hand sped like a snake toward the fleeing mare, danced across the path of her forefeet.

She jumped—but right into the loop.

Des set his booted feet in the grass.

The rope sang taut.

Estrellita, her forefeet in the air, fell in a long sliding drop to the soft grass.

Des sped up the rope, hand over hand, keeping it taut.

"Easy, girl," he soothed.

In seconds he stood over her. Then flipping the rope

across her body, he knelt to hold her head so she couldn't rise. A moment more and he had the rope around her neck—a hackamore fashioned on her soft nose.

"Okay, girl," he said, releasing her head, and standing erect.

Estrellita clambered to her feet.

"Seventeen and one-half minutes!" sang Janet.

"Great, and you win," Harry said, coming up to slap Des generously on his shoulders.

"Nice work, Des," another voice said. "Quick thinking, and no harm done to the mare. That's the kind of stuff that'll get Rocket."

Des swung to face Lynn MacLean, to see his Buick beyond him.

"Hello, Lynn," he said, slipping the rope from Estrellita and watching her run nickering back to the herd. "It was just an idea." And one that wouldn't do for Rocket. There'd be too much power in Rocket's forelegs for him to throw, Des suddenly realized.

"Yeah," Lynn scooped Janet, dog and all, into his big arms, then faced Des. "Well, here's another one, and it may call for some fast thinking—nursemaiding a carload of steers up to Broken Arrow is no cinch."

Des looked at Lynn. Lynn caught on fast—it was probably why he'd written about Rocket.

"When do I start?" Des asked. He couldn't keep his mind off that great gold horse sweeping across Soda Springs Flats.

"Tonight," Lynn said, walking back to put a foot on the running board of his car. "I'm buying the steers from the *Circle C.* They'll be loaded about dark. I'll pick you up at eight o'clock and drive you into Magrath, put you on the freight, then drive overland to Broken Arrow myself—I've got some places to call on my way home. That's why I want you to take the dogies."

"Okay," Des, who had followed Lynn, nodded.

Suddenly Lynn faced Des, after dropping Janet to the grass.

"There's more to this than just a train ride with a load of bawlin' steers," he said, gravely. "That stallion's wild—probably's never had a rope on. And then, there's the ride up. You'll meet plenty of characters on the caboose. Maybe a Mexican named El Gato. He'll be bringing some Brahmin steers to Lethbridge for the Stampede. Sure you want to go?"

The look in Des' dark eyes sent Lynn sliding under the wheel of his car.

"Eight o'clock, sure." He nodded. "I'll see your mother then."

He put the car in gear, kicked the motor over and let in the clutch. A moment more and he was a dust cloud on the feeder road leading to the new gravel highway.

Des gently coiled his lariat—the rope that was to go with him on his hazardous attempt to catch Rocket.

"Got to get goin'," he whispered. "Got a thousand things to do—pack my war bag, my bedroll." He walked toward the barn and into the harness room, his mind on Soda Springs Flats, and the big Palomino horse that called it his range.

"Here's your watch, Des," Janet whispered. Coming in, she strapped it back on Des' lean wiry wrist. "Oh— Des, are you afraid?" Her skinny arms flung around his neck, and all but squeezed off his wind.

Des gulped and pried her loose, he was more scared than he dared to show. But suddenly something within him set like steel.

"Naw," he said. "Now scram. I've got to pack my stuff."

Janet slipped out the door to find her puppy. And Des, with Harry to help, went to work. And as he worked, he remembered about meeting El Gato, and wondered.

CHAPTER II

EL GATO

WHEN LYNN DROVE UP THE WINDING TRAIL TO THE *Twin Anchor* that night, Des was still wondering about the Mexican.

"Ready?" Lynn sprang from the car and came over to Mrs. Harmon. "Glad we fixed things with Hawkins," he said. "Even if he did shave a week off the time he'd postpone the sale."

Des' heart began to thud. Three weeks to ride two hundred miles on a train, catch a wild stallion, and then ride him home—across country.

"Yeah, ready," he managed to say to Lynn, piling his bedroll and saddle in the back. "I'll keep my war bag up here," he said, getting into the front seat. Panic swept through him there in the dark, with the wind blowing off the Rockies. A hunch filled him, too, that a test lay ahead of him with Lynn's carload of steers.

He hid his panic by busily stowing the lunch his mother had put up for him in the front seat beside him.

"Good-bye, son," Mrs. Harmon's lips met his as she leaned into the car to kiss him. "I put in clean socks and underwear."

Des was to remember the strength of that kiss through the grueling days ahead.

Janet suddenly wailed, "Don't go!"

Des laughed, as Harry slapped his back. "Lucky!" he said enviously.

In a moment Des was in Lynn's car and speeding down the prairie trail to the highway.

As they turned onto it, and the crunch of the tires on the gravel sang a monotonous song, Lynn turned to the boy.

"I don't want to scare you, Des," he said, watching a jack rabbit, hypnotized by the light, dash into it and run lightly ahead of the car. "But there're other men who'd like to have Rocket. He'd bring a thousand dollars as a sire for some California breeder's herd— O'Brien of Santa Barbara, Mrs. Anthony of Sierra Madre."

Des drew in his breath sharply.

Lynn grinned. "So, just take it easy. Listen more than you talk. And don't tip your hand on this capture."

"Cat's got nursey's tongue," Des said, feeling very afraid inside.

"Right!"

They drove along in silence till Lynn turned down the main street of Magrath, then on down along the car tracks to the siding.

A freight train stood there, the engine puffing at the head of eighteen boxcars, two slatted stock cars, and a dinky little caboose, funnier than usual with its little cupola with windows all around.

Lynn drove down to the freight car by the stockyards. Des got out almost before the Buick stopped rolling. Lynn followed.

"Another thing, Des. I didn't tell you, but Mather of the *Circle C* says there's a big scheme on to round up all those Soda Springs wild horses for pet food."

"Put Rocket in a can?" Des exclaimed, memorizing the number of Lynn's stock car: Canadian Pacific Railway, 235864, painted in white on the side of the car.

Lynn nodded. "But it'll take 'em a week to get organized. So it's up to you to take these dogies up there and keep busy."

Des felt impatient to start rolling. He stuck his head up to look through the slats. The smell of the cattle, the gentle sniffing of them, and their horns rattling hollowly in the dark, gave Des the creeps.

He covered his feeling by turning to Lynn. "You said it," he agreed.

The engine up ahead gave a short sharp whistle.

"At the stations, get out of the caboose and come up alongside," Lynn explained. "If a crittur's down, prod him up."

The train, releasing its air brakes with a hiss, shunted forward, then back, then forward.

The brakie up ahead waved his little lantern in a half arc, and the train began to crawl slowly forward.

"That's all," Lynn added, as they walked quickly back toward the caboose. "I'll expect you day after to-morrow. You'll have to feed and water in Lethbridge —be careful!"

Des nodded, his eye on the comic little car that was to be his home for the next few days.

As it came gliding toward him, he put his hand on the catch-rail, his foot on the bottom step and swung aboard. A thrill passed through him. On the way. A real cowman bound for Broken Arrow with a load of steers under his charge.

"I'll take your stuff," Lynn called.

Des waved.

"Be careful!" Lynn's voice was back in the dark by now.

Des nodded again, then, skipping up the three steps to the rear platform, opened the caboose door and stepped inside—to bump into a little swarthy-faced man in a trick suit of black, with silver trimming, and a black sombrero with studs of the same metal on the crown and around the wide brim.

"Hello, puncher," he said in a soft complimentary

drawl. "I am El Gato—The Cat." He swept his sombrero off a head of curly black hair. "A gift of Señor Reyes of the *Sombrero Ranch* on the banks of the Rio de Sonora in Dorado, Mexico. The sombrero is his horse brand—on the neck."

Des couldn't help smiling with El Gato. His greeting was so friendly.

"This Señor Reyes, he breeds Palominos," El Gato said, in disgust. "Those cream-colored riffraffs!"

El Gato's tone caught Des off guard.

"Cream-nothings!" he defended hotly. "You haven't seen Rocket up on Soda Springs Flats. Or Estrellita on my Dad's ranch—" His voice trailed off before the sudden light in El Gato's black eyes. He knew he'd said too much. But before El Gato's apology, Des felt easier.

"So—then I am sorry I said that. Rocket, eh?"

Des barely nodded, so El Gato changed the subject.

"I am taking Burma cattle—bucking cattle—to the Lethbridge Stampede—the Red Cross Benefit July first." Then he added in distress, "I heard the Lethbridge stockyards are in quarantine for mange. That all stock will be held for two weeks."

Des fell into a second trap.

"Boy!" He started, then stared through the rear caboose window, forgetting El Gato. "Maybe I can get Lynn's car set out at the Raymond siding?"

"You are taking cattle too," El Gato asked, softly. "Too bad."

"To Soda Springs—I mean Broken Arrow."

"Ah—you take the cattle up, then you try for Rocket, eh? This wild stallion will be for your ranch?"

Des caught his breath.

But El Gato was off on a long speech about his own youth. "Ah—I had the best horse in all Mexico. I get him back on a ranch, here in Canada. He is black and slim like the snake—La Culebra!"

"You say you are getting him back. You've found out where he is?" Des asked.

But the train, slowing for their first town of Raymond, saved El Gato from answering.

Des got up to go and inspect his car.

El Gato followed.

"Everything's okay," Des said, peering through the slats at the steers all standing quietly, but shuffling as the car swayed with their weight.

"You would like to see my Brahmins?" El Gato said, leading the way to his car and politely striking a match.

Des peered between the slats at big brindle steers with a single hump along their backs.

"For the rodeos—stampedes, you say here in Canada," El Gato explained. "They will be plenty rough on the ride, yes? But the prizes"—El Gato waved his thin hands—"a silver-trimmed saddle for the bucking horse. Five hundred dollars for the calf roping."

Des instinctively felt the rope on his arm. And he wondered. That five hundred dollars would come in mighty handy.

The train started to move.

"I think we'd better get back," Des said.

"No, there is time—plenty time." El Gato put a detaining hand on Des' arm. "We will make of it a game—to see how fast the train can go and we catch it."

The train was picking up speed.

Des looked sharply at El Gato. Not a thing in his face but friendliness, and the high good spirits of a pal.

The boxcars slid past Des.

He tore loose from El Gato and ran down the track.

El Gato followed, outdistancing him.

Des felt something trip him. He fell headlong, cutting his cheek on the cinders. As he sprang up, the caboose loomed, coming—

El Gato swung on, then turned on the bottom step. As Des made a grab for the rail, El Gato seemed to slip, knocking Des free of the train. It began to glide away into the dark, leaving Des there beside the rails.

For a second Des, with the wind knocked out of him, couldn't yell. But then he did.

A brakeman appeared behind El Gato, and taking

in the situation at a glance, leaned past El Gato and waved the engine down with his lantern.

"Watch it, kid," he said, as Des ran up, panting. "After this give yourself plenty of time."

Des clambered up the steps, past an apologetic El Gato and into the caboose.

Well, he knew where he was with El Gato now. Or did he? El Gato was so contrite. And, during the next three stations, did not stir from the caboose.

And when the freight, in the early morning hours, chugged into the Lethbridge freight yards, El Gato helped him unload. Swinging off the caboose, stretching, and saying regretfully to Des, "Ah—the end of the road for me. We will unload, yes? Me to turn my steers over to the Lethbridge Big-Shots. You to feed and water, then, *pouf*—we see each other no more."

Des nodded, soberly, and politely said, "Tough luck." Then he sat down on the edge of the loading platform to wait for the freight engine to spot his car at the un-loading chute. It was half dark. Stars still shone faintly in the paling night sky when the freight engine finally came chugging down, spotted El Gato's car, waited while he and Des put the plank floor across the space, swung the two big whitewashed gates into place, and opening the cattle-car door, whooped the big brindle steers down into the corral.

"Boy!" Des' eyes widened at the size of them. "Brass knobs on their horns."

"To keep the riders from getting gored when thrown," El Gato explained. "Without them, bang, the steer wheel and run the horn right through the rider."

Des couldn't help shivering, and he was glad when the freight engine spotted his own car.

"I help you," El Gato said. "You help me."

Des nodded, and they went through the same process as with the Brahmin steers.

In half an hour, the forty steers Lynn was going to fatten for the Canadian Government watered at a trough on one side of their feed pen, then munched hay from the rack beside it.

El Gato looked at the pile of dry hay, then out over the lines of pens. "A fire would not be so much fun," he said, once more eying the hay.

"No!" Des agreed.

El Gato added, "The mange quarantine was a scare and would have been no fun, either I am sorry to make that mistake and worry you."

Des shrugged.

"Now, perhaps you will forgive me better if we go and I buy you some breakfast—flapjacks and milk, maybe?"

Des was plenty hungry. He'd eaten his lunch at midnight. And he had to eat before the train pulled out around nine o'clock. But he didn't want anything more to do with El Gato.

"I'll get mine later," he said. "Don't wait for me, and thanks just the same."

"Of course, well, I will say good-bye, friend. And good luck with the Palomino."

Des couldn't help flushing. It was against his nature to turn down a guy who seemed as friendly as El Gato.

"Thanks," he said. "And good luck to you." He shook hands with the Mexican, then sat down on the edge of the feed rack to watch the steers eat.

He guessed they'd weigh around six hundred pounds now. Turned out on Soda Springs Flats in June, by November, when the snow began to fly, they'd weigh around eight hundred—a nice bunch of beef for the army.

At length, Des shivered, and drew his leather jumper around his slender shoulders. He recoiled his rope and hung it carefully across his left arm, glancing hungrily across the tracks to a neon sign that read, *Royal Cafe*. Everything in Canada was Royal this, Empress that. The boy grinned and passed his tongue across his dry lips. A cup of coffee would hit the spot right now—and maybe a dish of hot oatmeal.

He glanced down at his watch; five o'clock. He needn't be gone more than fifteen minutes.

Des made his way out of the corral and across the tracks to the café. Shoving open the door, and walking through it, he caught his breath. For there, on a stool at the counter, sat El Gato.

"Hello, puncher," he said, with the same smile that he'd used in the caboose. He turned to the heavy-set man behind the counter. "My friend," he explained, draining his coffee cup, then slid from the stool to his dainty booted feet. "You will feed him—some flapjacks and milk, for which I will pay."

"That will be a dollar and eighty cents with yours," the man said, counting up with heavy moving lips.

"Here's mine," Des said, tossing a dollar bill on the counter. "I'll pay my own way."

El Gato shrugged and without another word slipped out into the half-light of dawn.

The man behind the counter studied the door through which El Gato had slipped so quickly.

"Seemed in kind of a hurry, your friend," he mused.

Something clicked in Des' mind, and he heard again as plainly as though El Gato spoke the words beside him. "A fire would be no fun, either—"

He leaped to the counter and pointed to a stack of doughnuts. "Gimme those," he said. "And a bottle of milk—quick!"

In less than a minute, Des had slipped through the

door after El Gato. Moving softly across the tracks to the yards, Des felt he was about to face a nasty situation. He rounded one end of the corral and opened the gate. A dark slim shape was bent low, over by the end of the feed rack, a cigarette glowing against his swarthy face.

Des quietly set his doughnuts and milk on the corral's dusty ground, and with deft hands flipped a loop in his lariat.

Now El Gato stood between the hay rack and the water trough. His slim dark hand raised to flip the lighted cigarette into the dry hay. A soft laugh escaped his crafty lips. And the butt flew to its mark.

Des took two steps forward, his rope sailed through the air and the loop settled over El Gato's shoulders and down his slim body.

Des jerked the rope taut. Jerked again.

"Caramba!" El Gato sputtered from the water trough.

Des ran across and with his hands scooped water from the trough to the smoldering hay.

In a moment, the danger was passed.

"Santa Maria!" El Gato climbed from the trough, dripping like a water spaniel.

Des, grinning inside, now that the fire was out, picked up El Gato's hat.

"I'm so sorry," he said, contritely. "I thought you were a crazy bum trying to burn up my dogies."

El Gato snatched the hat, his eyes burning with fury. He took a menacing step toward Des. But just then the light of the freight engine flashed into his face and the brakie, swinging from the cowcatcher, yelled, "Hey, kid, we're pulling out on a faster schedule. Let's get those dogies loaded."

Des sang out, "Okay! My friend here and I'll load 'em, pronto."

He turned to El Gato. "How about it, friend?"

Solemnly El Gato nodded, and in tense silence helped Des move the cattle back into the stock car.

When they were all inside and the door locked, Des went back to get his doughnuts and milk, then walked toward the little red caboose, now plainly visible in the clear morning light.

A meadow lark whistled from a corral post. A red truck drove by with a load of hay. Des, calling on all the high school Spanish he knew, held out his hand to El Gato.

"*Saludas amigo,*" he said. "Which in English means, with me, "Good-bye forever!""

He dropped El Gato's hand and swung down the tracks and aboard the caboose bound for Broken Arrow and Rocket. But the look in El Gato's eyes that followed him told Des that it wasn't good-bye forever. They'd meet again, he knew.

CHAPTER III

ATTEMPTED CAPTURE

THE FREIGHT RUMBLED INTO BROKEN ARROW AT FOUR IN the afternoon of the second day. Des slipped from the caboose almost before the train stopped rolling. A brisk wind from the Rockies off to the west made him grab for his Stetson as he stared at a group of shacks making up the town of Broken Arrow.

"Look like they'd been dumped from a plane," he decided.

"Hi!" Lynn greeted him from the Buick, then stared at Des' cut cheek.

Des, piling in beside him, let it pass, and El Gato too. That was history. What he was interested in was the Palomino stallion.

"Is Rocket still there?" he demanded, eagerly.

Lynn nodded, grinning, and drove down to the stockyards, beating the engine, which was spotting Des' car at the unloading chutes, by less than a minute.

Two riders sat their horses, waiting—an old man with stooped shoulders and a slouch Stetson, and an Indian boy on a blue roan.

"Jim Pyne—an old Indian scout—and White Cloud,"

Lynn explained. "They'll haze the dogies out to the ranch—Come over here, White Cloud."

Des watched the slim boy slip from his horse and, with that effortless, tireless slouch of the Indian, walk over to them.

"This is Des Harmon, White Cloud," Lynn said. "He come catch Rocket—Cream-Horse-That-Goes-Like-Bullet!"

White Cloud's expressionless black eyes fell on Des, making him squirm.

"White Cloud go Indian School," he grunted, at length. "Learn, two times two make five—you no ketchum Rocket."

Lynn chuckled.

White Cloud stooped to the prairie grass and with a long brown forefinger traced a line.

"White man trail Rocket like this—no ketchum."

"That was Tom Story, last year," Lynn explained to Des. "He wore out three saddle horses, then gave up."

White Cloud scooped a little hole in the sod, then covered it with grass blades.

"Rocket come, smell hole white man dug. Give heap big jump! Mistapoot!" White Cloud's arm traced a big arc toward the blue Porcupine Hills off to the west.

Lynn nodded to Des.

"That's about the truth. Mistapoot is Blood Indian for scrammed. And that's what Rocket did."

White Cloud stood erect, fixing stolid eyes again on Des, and shaking his big bony head.

"White man try run Rocket down. Night and day, always chase big gold horse." His shoulders dropped showing great disgust. "Always Rocket ahead like big gold bullet. You go home—save time, save money, save Rocket make you big chump!"

Des could only think of one thing: to get moving.

"Glad to meet White Cloud," he said. His lips twitched. "Two times two make four—I catch Rocket!"

He turned, as the freight engine bumped to a stop, his eyes meeting Lynn's.

"Okay, White Cloud," Lynn said. "Let's get these dogies unloaded."

Pyne got stiffly off his bay, and with the high-heeled stiffness of an old cowman, hobbled over to where Lynn and Des already had the chute gates swung around, the door open, and the steers jamming down the chute to the whitewashed corral.

Lynn walked through them and swung open the gate leading to the prairie.

"Okay, Pyne, you and White Cloud get rollin'. Take em easy—and bring 'em right into *Broken Arrow*

Ranch. We brand before we kick 'em out to graze."

"Yes, sir," Pyne said dryly. The first words, Des noticed, that he'd spoken.

The two riders whooped the cattle into a bunch and started off across the prairie, stretching southwest clean to the Porcupine Hills.

Des threw his head back and took a deep breath. He ached from his long train ride in the cramped caboose.

"Some country," he said. "And now for Rocket!"

He hopped into the Buick, leaned forward as the car started, and fixed his eyes on the trail ahead.

"Boy!" he breathed. "I can hardly wait. I'll write Dad the minute I ride Rocket into the *Twin Anchor.*"

"Counting your chickens before they're hatched, aren't you?" Lynn asked, dryly, giving the car the gun.

Des sat with his coiled lariat on his arm. His eyes that grew brighter as the miles skimmed under the car scarcely left the hills ahead. Ten miles, fifteen, twenty— The sun slid low on the horizon, banking behind Old Chief Peak, turning the sky to a flaming red.

They topped a rise and suddenly Soda Springs Flats lay before them.

Des' eyes swept the fifty-square-mile stretch of prairie. Hardly a knoll on it—just flat grazing land with an alkali spring in the center.

He put his trembling hand on the side of the car and

gripped it tight, for there, off in the distance, he caught
the outline of a band of maybe fifteen horses—little
black specks on the prairie, with one lighter speck off
to one side.

"Gosh!" Des thought he couldn't stand it, the way
his heart thumped. "Rocket, and his band of mares!"

They drove along, the road leading straight toward
the springs.

"We go within half a mile of them," Lynn explained.
"But when we get that close, Rocket won't be there."

But he was.

Suddenly, Des, drawn by some instinctive impulse,
put his hand on Lynn's arm.

He just said, "Stop the car a minute, will you, Lynn?"

Then, when the car rolled to a halt, and before Lynn
could take in what he was about, Des was out of the car
and walking across the short dry prairie wool, straight
toward Rocket.

He paid no attention to the possible danger of being
pounded to death under Rocket's black hoofs, or to
Lynn's shouts of "Come back!"

A quarter of a mile, with little spurts of dust puffing
up under his riding boots, Des walked on.

He could see Rocket close, now, his great head thrown
back, his silver mane flying, his platinum tail streaming
out behind, as he marshaled his mares for flight.

Des fixed his eyes on the pale stallion. He began to talk before he should get too close. Soft soothing words—

"Hi, boy! Hi, old timer! This is no place for you. You've got work to do in this world. Life isn't all holiday."

Rocket, with that tireless rocking-chair pace, wove back and forth in front of his mares, now. Fifteen of them—some blacks, two bays, and a pinto or two. Not the stuff Rocket should be in the same pasture with.

Des held his breath. Any moment Rocket might light out, now. He slowed down, keeping his rope tight to his side.

He kept on talking. "Hi, Rocket. You'll be dog-meat if you don't listen. Come on, boy. Come on."

Suddenly, Rocket sent his band of mares scurrying to a rise beyond the springs. He stood on the point of it and trumpeted shrilly, sending his challenge off into the gathering night.

Des was right at the springs, now, clear cool water bubbling from the ground and running off into a small lake.

"Hi, boy," Des called. He pursed his lips and called Rocket with a soft coaxing whistle.

Suddenly, Rocket came on. With that racking, ground-eating pace, his head high, his wide eyes flashing, he bore down on the helpless Des.

Des braced his feet in the soft muddy ground. He clutched his rope tight and waited.

A hundred yards Rocket came on. It seemed to Des that he would knock him to the ground and beat him into it with those flying hoofs.

Des thought of his Dad out on that destroyer, the way his big blond face would light up when he read of Rocket's capture. He braced his feet and hung on.

Lynn honked his horn. Des could see him standing up in the car. He had Rocket covered with his rifle. Des signaled him to put up his gun, and his eyes went back to Rocket.

The horse raced to within twenty feet of Des. He stopped, his great hoofs plowing deep into the soft muddy ground. He began circling Des, tossing his head, his eyes glowing and deep with question.

Suddenly, Des wasn't afraid anymore. For the great gold horse stopped, and fixed his big brown eyes on Des'. Something seemed to flow between them.

"The Golden Mustang!" Des whispered. He said it aloud: "Golden Mustang—come on, boy. You're mine."

Rocket tossed his head, uncertainly. He grew very still, and in his big eyes Des saw memory take hold.

Des uncoiled his rope.

"Rope—you know, boy," he said softly.

Rocket stood like a golden statue. Suddenly he began

to tremble, then, with a shrill trumpet of alarm, swerved his big huge-barrelled body and with forelegs like pistons, drove for the hills.

Des stood swallowing, his mind racing. Then he smiled, and with a quick circling movement of his arm spread the rope around.

"Get used to the smell of it, boy," he said. "And I'll be back, tomorrow night—same time, same station."

He walked back to the car, a slow fire of excitement and wonder for the horse he'd seen burning within him.

"Of all the fool stunts," Lynn exploded. "He might have tramped you right into Soda Springs!"

Des, without replying, climbed in beside Lynn. One big question mark filled his mind. Rocket would let him slip the rope over his head in time—but would it be before the pet-food men came?

He clenched his fists and sat straight and stiff and planning, as Lynn started the car and drove on to top the rise leading out of Soda Springs Flats, then down to *Broken Arrow Ranch*.

He stopped before the little log cabin, to the left of the bigger log cabin that was the barn, and Des climbed slowly from the car and lugged his war bag and bedroll into the cabin. He wished it was tomorrow evening, and he was at Soda Springs. A fever filled him. A fever and a firm determination to get Rocket ahead of the roundup.

CHAPTER IV

DISASTER

THE NEXT MORNING, UNDER DES' RED-AND-WHITE PLAID shirt, that determination burned bright as ever.

He gulped his breakfast of pancakes, bacon and canned milk with one eye on the cloud bank over Old Chief Peak, the other on a bag of rock salt standing just inside the pantry door.

"This is the day I'll take him," he told himself, softly.

"Day you catchum wind." White Cloud, sitting opposite, grunted. "You stay for help 'em brand dogies. More fun. More sure Rocket no makum you big chump."

Pyne said nothing, his faded blue eyes on the plate he cleaned in silence.

"Okay, boys." Lynn slid back his kitchen chair on the bare pine floor. "Let's get those dogies branded and out to grass." He strode toward the door, hat in hand.

He turned to Des, his eyes concerned, but sparkling. "Take anything you need around here—ropes—anything else. Old Blue's in the barn. Help yourself."

Des knew what he meant: not to go out there to face Rocket on foot again.

"I'll be okay, Lynn," he promised, putting up a front.

He scarcely knew what the great cream horse really had wanted, coming back to circle him like that.

But he got a little better idea two hours later, when he reached Soda Springs on foot and grinned down at his rope. Rocket had been there in the night and, seeing what the horse had done, Des couldn't help laughing softly.

"So Rocket was a kidder, was he?" Des' eyes followed the course of the rope.

"Oh yeah——?" it seemed to say. Des could picture his big black hoofs striking at the snakelike rope. And suddenly he felt as though he'd come a little closer to Rocket. He got a feeling, too, that the Palomino might have played with some Mexican boy's rope when he'd been a colt.

Des heard a noise behind him, and wheeled sharply, and there, standing silently, his great brown eyes fixed on Des, stood Rocket.

Des jumped, then colored.

"Hey, guy," he groused, feeling the red climb up from his shirt collar to spread over his face. "What's the idea?"

Rocket snorted, then stepped nearer, stretching out his long graceful neck. His platinum mane fell down along his sleek gold coat.

Des caught his breath at the beauty of this horse. So solid, and yet so slender. He marveled at his heart girth, and the stamina the horse must have. Des could scarcely breathe for the longing within him to own this horse for always.

"So you want salt, eh?" he whispered, reaching inside his shirt and bringing out a lump of it.

With his movement, Rocket swung around and paced away.

Des sensed again the feeling he couldn't get rid of, that everything Rocket did would be the last time he'd do it. Maybe he'd pull up stakes and quit the range— drift on north up into the Peace River—perhaps clean up to Alaska.

He stood quite still, his eyes on Rocket's mares standing on a knoll off to the left. He began to call the stallion, his heart in his mouth, his voice husky with eagerness. "Come, boy! Come, boy! Come, boy!"

Rocket paced down to him, coming with that headlong ground-covering gait that left Des weak at the knees. To be on that broad satin back! To sail over the prairie on him!

He met Rocket with the salt and the rope coiled and ready to throw.

Rocket looked at the salt, then spotted the rope. With a snort, he stopped beyond the range of Des' throwing arm, his hoofs tossing loose soft dirt disdainfully. For a full minute, he stood there, eyes on Des, neck bowed.

Then he shrilled out his disdain and with creamy tail held
in an arch, wheeled and fled for his mares, marshaled
them with masterly little runs and bites on their rumps,
and disappeared on the horizon.

Des felt foolish, and slightly sick. He turned and
walked slowly back to *Broken Arrow*. He was defeated
for the moment, but still determined to capture Rocket
for his very own. To ride, to take back to the *Twin
Anchor*.

But, along with the determination, he got the feeling,
during the evening, and all that night, that Rocket would
quit him cold, that the big horse was angry and wouldn't
be there for days.

However, the next morning, after he had covered the
five miles out to Soda Springs, there was Rocket walking
along with him. Off to one side, it was true, but undeni-
ably keeping pace with him.

"Sort of convoying me, eh, *amigo?*" Des asked.

Rocket, at the sound of the Spanish word, pricked up
his pointed ears.

Des tried it again, calling on his slim Spanish.
"Amigo—"

It got to be a game—a game that Rocket played so
long as Des didn't try to touch him. Rock salt from his
hand? Sure. And dried apples—his velvety lips nibbling
gently at them? Okay.

But the game had to end as the days passed. The pet-food men were closing in.

"They landed in Broken Arrow today," Lynn reported the sixth night. "Long lean guy named James is straw boss." He leaned his arms on the dinner table and took a big drink of coffee from his cup. "They've bought up five miles of fence posts and wire." Lynn set his cup down and mimicked James' drawl. "I aim to build a squeeze fence, then haze them cayuses into a trap at the north end of Soda Flats."

A fine dew came out on Des' forehead. He speared another of Lynn's baking-powder biscuits with a shaking fork. "But, he can't do that!" he protested.

"Can't he?" They were the first words Pyne had spoken in two days. "Them Sody Flats is owned by an Eastern Syndicate. He can fence 'em, round up twenty cars of cayuses, and be gone before anybody'd get wise."

Des gulped. "And Rocket along with them."

Pyne nodded, adding dryly, "You'd better make tracks with the hoss catchin', son. James may even take a notion to fence off Soda Springs to Rocket. Thirst'd make him easy to take."

Des forgot to eat his biscuit.

He slipped from the chair and going into his bedroom crawled into his bedroll and lay tossing anxiously until at last he fell asleep. With the first streak of dawn, he got up and, dressing quickly, slipped out to the barn, saddled Old Blue and headed north. Maybe he could get James to quit? Maybe it was a false alarm?

But riding to the north end of Soda Flats, he checked Old Blue on a rise, staring down at two men with spades and crowbars setting cedar posts. They worked from a V, setting the posts two rods apart. And at the V, a tall man, whom Des instantly recognized as James, worked on the posts that would make a round corral.

Des shoved Old Blue down to stand before him. But before he could open his mouth, James opened up.

"You the kid that's tryin' to ketch that gold stallion?" he drawled, fixing cold blue eyes on Des.

Des nodded.

James set a seven-foot post in the hole he'd dug, slid in some soft dirt and took up his tamper.

"Then, you'd best make it snappy," he said, beginning long powerful strokes with the iron bar. "Rate we're settin' these posts, we'll be roundin' up in four days."

"Four days—" Des whispered. He could see by James' eyes that there was no use arguing. But he had to try. "You wouldn't ship a swell horse like Rocket?" Des demanded.

James stopped to lean on his tamper. His blue eyes followed the horizon above Soda Springs Flats.

"Kid," he said, "I take orders from a company. I got to shoot square with them—and their orders are to ship any stuff I round up off Soda Springs range."

He moved on to set another post with deadly speed.

Des swung Old Blue toward home. Well, he had four days. A lot could be done in that time. He set Old Blue at a steady lope, his mind on Rocket. He wasn't licked yet. Not as long as he had legs and a head.

He rode Blue into the barn, unsaddled him and stepped across the barn sill to go to the house. A rock there seemed to come from nowhere and get under Des' boot heel. He felt a blinding pain shoot through his ankle and dropped to the ground.

Lynn came from the branding corral and carried Des into his bunk.

"Just a sprain," he said, peeling off Des' boot and running a deft hand along the ankle, which was already turning blue. "It'll be okay in about four days—I'll get some hot water."

Four days—just the time he'd counted on to get Rocket ahead of James, Des figured. He took hold of the side of the pine board at the edge of his bunk, and lay thinking of Rocket—of his terror at being corraled—of—

He dropped off to sleep. And suddenly, it was morning. And then, another morning, and another. And, boy, today his ankle felt well. Peering out the window, Des saw that it was a fine day.

He stepped to the floor. His ankle didn't hurt when he tried his weight on it. And he could get his boot on—

He raced through breakfast. Coiling his rope over his arm, he stepped outside.

Great fleecy clouds hung over the Rockies. A light wind blew dust in his face. He tasted it—glad to be on his feet. Everything was great—for off to the north, he made out a bunch of tiny specks on a hill. One speck, a little lighter than the rest, set his heart bounding. Rocket! This was the day. He felt it.

He recoiled his rope with great care. It responded, almost alive in the way it lay along his arm.

"Well, it's now or never, Lynn," he said, as the puncher came outside to stand by him.

"No ketchum," White Cloud said, turning black expressionless eyes on him.

Pyne, with that hobbling gait of the puncher afoot, moved wordlessly off toward the barn.

Lynn turned to stare at Des. "How about all of us giving you a hand, today? Maybe, by taking shifts we can run him down?"

"No ketchum," White Cloud grunted. "Him like

wind—you run, wind always ahead—always a-h-e-a-d.
Mistap-o-oot!" He waved his right arm in a big arc,
then moved after Pyne.

"That's as good an answer as I know," Des said.
"Unless I can slip a rope on Rocket with his consent and
bring him in, I guess it's no go."

"I'll run you a ways, anyhow. Save your ankle," Lynn
said.

Des nodded.

Lynn went to get his Buick.

Together, in silence, they rode north.

Two miles up the trail, they sighted James and six
other riders fanning off to the south.

"They'll start at the south end and work the whole
Soda Flats band north," Lynn said. "They'll make Soda
Springs about nightfall."

Des nodded. His breath was short. His heart pounded.

"Yes," he said, shortly. "They'll be just in time to see
me take Rocket."

They rode on in silence, till, a mile from Soda Springs,
Des slipped from the machine, thanked Lynn and, with
a great deal more assurance than he felt, walked toward
the deserted springs.

Then began a battle that lasted throughout the day—
for Rocket was there. Pacing down to see Des, playfully,

like a kid, kicking his shiny black heels into the air, dodging, turning, twisting—

"See me," he seemed to say.

It made Des sick inside.

"Come on, *amigo*," he said, his voice husky with the lump in his throat.

Rocket came. He put out his long neck. Nuzzled the apples. Bit one and chewed it.

Six times, in as many hours, he came close, only to scamper away the moment Des made a move toward his lariat.

Hours later, as the red sun dropped slowly over the snow-capped peaks in the west, and Rocket came again to Des, a haze of dust formed to the south.

"*Amigo!*" Des whispered, pleadingly. "They're coming—James and the other punchers. They'll kill you. Dead. Dead—get it?"

He moved closer to Rocket, taking his time, even with that cloud of fleeing horses bearing down on them. With the sun becoming a ball of fire, then dropping over the mountains, and the sky, first a red caldron, then becoming dimmer and dimmer.

"Come on, Rocket," he pleaded. "Come on, let me touch you."

The great horse seemed to sense something in Des' voice. His eyes softly on Des, he stood and let the lad put a hand on his neck, let him run it along to his steel-muscled satin shoulder.

"*Amigo!*" Des whispered. "*Amigo!*" He could hardly talk for the pain in his throat.

A moment more, and he'd have had his rope over Rocket's head. Been close to him, taming him. The horse seemed to trust him—

But the shouts of the riders swelled behind him. It rose to a tumult. The pound of hundreds of sharp hoofs on the prairie filled the air, roared in Rocket's ears.

He flung his head into the air, his eyes watching the approaching horses. His ears twitched at the wild shouts of James and his men.

Des felt his great neck quiver, felt him give ground. He stepped with him, pleading, opening his rope.

Rocket, his coat wet with nervous sweat, snorted and backed away. He turned sideways, and started to pace away, slowly at first, his great legs moving like slow pistons gathering speed for a long race.

Des felt the wonderful play of muscles in his neck where he grasped his mane, along his barrel side as it brushed his slight body.

"*Amigo,*" he pleaded. "The rope—let me slip it on."

But Rocket snorted again. His legs in that peculiar rocking-chair roll, beat faster.

Des knew a moment of anguish, terror that matched

this great horse's. He ran alongside him, his breath coming in sobs, pleading, *"Amigo,* stop! *Amigo,* trust me."

Rocket plunged on.

Des pulled harder on his silver mane. He felt his legs leave the ground, felt himself swept along. Rocket didn't kick at him, but paced on.

Suddenly, Des got a wild idea. Gathering his strength, he grasped the mane tighter, gave a big spring and landed square astride that big barrel body speeding off into the dark.

He felt Rocket quiver, sensed that the great stallion was gathering his body to buck. Then, suddenly, with the whole of Soda Springs before him, he stretched out into that tireless pacing gait that carried them away from James and his pack. And up ahead of the band, then west and into the clear—

On a hilltop miles from James, and behind him, Des brought Rocket to a halt.

A great elation filled him.

"Amigo, you are mine," he whispered in the starlight. "Mine."

Still astride Rocket, he ran his hand down along the sleek sweat-drenched neck under the silver mane.

Then something seemed to freeze within him. His fingers went on, tracing out the outlines of a small cunningly hidden brand: the sombrero!

CHAPTER V

TREACHERY

Des sat on the panting horse, his mind a big question mark. It looked as though he'd won Rocket just to lose him to his owner, Señor Don Reyes of Mexico.

But his fingers outlined the sombrero brand once more —and found a bar beneath it. What was that bar?

Des slipped to the soft spring grass and eased the lariat over Rocket's slim pointed ears. There was a lot to be decided yet, and Rocket was his for now anyway— maybe, always.

Deftly, Des put a half hitch over Rocket's soft nose, then another up through this and over his ears.

Boy, what a horse! Rocket came to him when he started to walk away. Broken to lead! Des whistled softly there in the dark. Rocket must have had some boy for a pal when he was a colt.

Des grasped his mane and with a quick spring mounted and rode Rocket the six miles back to *Broken Arrow Ranch*.

Lynn came out whistling and, putting out a hand, exclaimed, "Look at that heart girth and chest—those legs!"

49

Rocket backed off, snorting.

Pyne came from the bunkhouse, a red ghost in his woolen underwear.

"Rope horse—best I ever seen," he snapped drily, then turned and picked his way back to the square of light that was the bunkhouse door.

"Ketchum—no keepum," White Cloud said, appearing suddenly in the darkness. "Maybe now, maybe two moons—Cream-Horse go, Mistapoot—"

Des silently shook his head, then rode Rocket down to the corral, put him inside, tossed him a forkful of prairie hay, then walked back to the house. And as he walked, a tempting thought came to him.

Over a supper of bacon and beans with cold soda biscuits and coffee, he sat staring at the iron stove. Something inside him prompted, "That's a mighty little brand up there under Rocket's mane, where nobody'd see it? Why don't you forget it—ride him on home to the *Twin Anchor* and forget it?"

Des shifted his tired body in the straight kitchen chair. Maybe he was a chump to say anything about it? Maybe, if he just rode Rocket home and kept him?

But his Dad's level eyes, gray and straight-shooting, rose before Des'. And his Mom's brown ones, so brave— Des got up abruptly.

"Lynn?" He stared across the room at Lynn, lacing a

saddle cinch with a whang-leather thong. "You got some stuff for me to write a letter?"

Lynn brought out an indelible pencil, a piece of brown paper and an envelope marked BROKEN ARROW POST OFFICE. In the corner it had a red three-cent stamp with King George the Sixth's picture on it.

Des sat down and wrote across the top of the paper:

Dear Señor Reyes:
I captured a Palomino horse with your brand on it—

He stopped, and, as he chewed the pencil, a plan popped into his head. The stampede at Lethbridge. The Red Cross Benefit show. He'd make it there just in time. Win the calf roping and the five-hundred-dollar prize. Then buy Rocket from Don Reyes.

He wrote on:

If you will come to Lethbridge, Stampede day, I will buy your horse or turn him over to you. There is not time for an answer. So, if you are not there, you will find me and the horse at my home on the Twin Anchor Ranch, at Magrath, Alberta.

Yours truly,
Desmond Harmon

Des got up and gently put the finished letter on the table. There, that cinched it. Rocket would be his—if he won him. And he had to win—

"Ketchum letter?" Lynn said, watching Des' face, but showing that he wasn't butting in.

Des nodded, smiling wanly at the letter addressed to Dorado, Mexico, then turned to roll in. Boy, was he tired?

In the silence that followed, Des didn't explain. Lynn would think he was a little weak in the head going up against experienced calf ropers at the stampede—Jim Fleet of the *Triangle Ranch* on his horse Diamond, El Gato, the Mexican cat, quick as lightning. Des' heart began to thump. Maybe he was crazy. But he had it to do. And the sooner he got started the better.

He stretched, got a drink of water from the dipper in the tin bucket by the stove, then moved on into the bedroom.

"Good night," he said, in the doorway, stretching again. He had five days to get to the stampede. It would keep him humping.

"I'll roll my bed in the morning, Lynn," he said. "Got to get on back."

Next morning, Des sat astride Rocket, who stood prancing, fighting his wide spade bit.

It was crisp and clear at five, with the sun just coming over the Sweet Grass Hills to the east. A meadow lark whistled on a fence post by the wire gate. A slight breeze

blew down from Crow's Nest Pass, riffling the cotton-
wood tree by the corner of the log cabin.

White Cloud saw the letter in Des' hand, and stepping
close, reached for it, his black eyes shining.

"Me educated—me mailum in Broken Arrow heap
soon."

Des hesitated. This letter to Don Reyes was important.
But, if White Cloud did mail it, it would cut miles off
his trip—he could cut due east.

"Okay, White Cloud," he said, handing the Indian
boy the letter. "You mail, sure?"

White Cloud nodded, and in less than a minute rode
Old Blue for Broken Arrow.

Des turned to Lynn.

"So long," he said, softly. "You've been swell."

"Skip it," Lynn handed him twenty dollars in one-
dollar bills. "Here's your pay for nurse-maidin' the
steers."

Des pocketed the money, his fingers trembling. Here
was his entry money for the calf roping.

"Don't ride after sundown," Lynn cautioned. "You've
got to cross the Blood Reserve and right by Robber's
Roost Ranch—there's a renegade outfit that knows
horseflesh. And they know plenty of Palomino breeders
through the states that'd give a cool thousand for
Rocket."

Des nodded, turning Rocket eastward and slightly south.

"So long, Lynn," he said, lightly touching Rocket with the rowels of his spurs.

"Good luck," Lynn called.

And Des rode Rocket out the wire gate, swung to the east, feeling strangely small against the sweep of prairie before him. The *Twin Anchor* seemed suddenly far away.

In Broken Arrow, there was another who meant to see that *Twin Anchor* was still farther away, and that Des wouldn't ever get Rocket there—a slim, dark man with a deceptive smile and a black sombrero hat.

"Ah—*buenos dias!!*" El Gato greeted White Cloud. For there was El Gato riding a slim black mare. "A letter?" He had ridden close to White Cloud and had it in his hands before White Cloud could gulp.

"Mailum for boy who captured Cream-Horse-That-Fades-Into-The-Night," White Cloud grunted. "You giveum back."

El Gato drew the letter free of White Cloud's clutching hand.

"To save you the trouble, I'll mail it," El Gato said. In his slim catlike hand, he held out a silver dollar.

White Cloud stolidly eyed the dollar, then El Gato.

"You sure mailum?" he grunted.

"*Si*," El Gato smiled, softly. "I am friend of this boy," he lied.

White Cloud seemed satisfied.

"Ugh! Heap good!" He took the dollar and rode on down Broken Arrow's single street, and toward a sign that said, DRUG STORE—FOUNTAIN.

El Gato rode toward the post office, till White Cloud disappeared inside the store, then swerved his horse and rode out of town. On the edge of it, he checked his horse and ripped open Des' letter to Don Reyes.

Minutes passed as he read it.

A freight train bumped cars on the siding. A young Indian squaw in a big white Hudson's Bay blanket with red and white and green bands rode by.

Suddenly, El Gato looked up from his letter.

"So," he said, softly, a crafty smile spreading over his dark face. "You have caught the Palomino for me, not Señor Reyes."

Tearing the letter into bits, he swerved his black mount east and slightly south. It would be a simple matter to ride ahead of Des and ambush him. The boy would be no match for El Gato. Soon the horse would be his, and he knew a man in Santa Barbara, California, who would pay a thousand dollars for a sire like that, and figure he had a bargain to boot.

El Gato put his horse to a ground-eating half-trot half-walk, that would carry him relentlessly toward Des.

Des rode along the open prairie. He had range sense, keeping a beeline for the Sweet Grass Hills and Leavings, on the banks of the St. Marys River.

Gophers sat like picket-pins on their dirt mounds, whistling, setting up a chattering as their age-old enemy, the chicken hawk, swooped low over the hills, sending them scurrying into their holes.

Herds of white-faced cattle grazed on the slopes, raising big brown eyes to stare at this boy who looked like an ant atop his big golden horse. Little white-faced calves bumped their mother's udders with blunt impatient noses, their tails thumping along the sleek ribs.

Des, out in the open, began training Rocket for the grueling trail ahead.

"*Amigo*," he said, "you must learn that a bit is something besides a thing to make you stop and start." He put his reins along the left side of Rocket's sleek neck. "That means go right," he said. "That's it!"

Rocket picked it up almost at once.

"Now—left. Now—right. Okay, boy." After half an hour, and without slackening his steady progress east, Des had taught Rocket to neck-rein. He topped a rise, and between two hills found a clear cold spring.

When he alighted to drink, he dropped Rocket's reins.
Rocket moved away, thinking to escape. The reins
fouled with his forefeet, jerking his mouth cruelly.

"Tough," Des said, rising and wiping his mouth. "But
it's the only way to make you know that to a cow-horse
dropped reins are the same as though you were tied to a
solid post."

He led Rocket up to the spring and watched him
shove his soft black nose deep into the bubbling water.
When Rocket had had enough, Des rode on.

Hours passed. When the sun cast a shadow directly
under Rocket's belly, Des dismounted, slipped Rocket's
bridle and, keeping hold of the hackamore rope, let the
big horse graze. Then, getting out the lunch Lynn had
put up, he ate the hard-boiled eggs and bacon between
slabs of white bread.

In twenty minutes, he bridled Rocket and rode on—
for Leavings was many miles away, and the sun had
already begun its journey to the western horizon.

It was four in the afternoon that Des rode down
through Belly River.

Rocket waded out into the stream, dropping his head
to drink, nuzzling the cold rushing water on his foamy
mouth. Then, filled up, he waded on toward the opposite
bank and up. It was a two-foot climb. Rocket leaped,
but Des' stirrup caught on a tree stump.

Rocket snorted, feeling the strange pull. In a panic, he bolted.

"Whoa! Cut it out—it's only a hung stirrup!"

But in a moment, Des felt the saddle give, heard the sound of his cotton cinch tearing, and before he could do anything about it, he lay piled with his saddle, while off a few feet distant, Rocket stood, trembling, but tied by his falling reins.

Des got up, ruefully eying his broken cinch.

"Now we're in for it," he said, walking over to Rocket. "Fifteen miles from Leavings, and—"

"Hello," a friendly voice said.

Des swung around to see a blond boy on a pinto pony branded with a big B-108 on his thigh. "Hello," he said, staring questioningly at the unfamiliar brand.

"Blood Indian brand, B for Blood. Each Indian has a number," the boy answered his unspoken query, and jumped lightly to the ground. "I'm Ron Stanley," he said, coming over to Des. "Dad runs the Agency at Stand-off, down the river a mile."

"Stand-off?" Des smiled quizzically at the name.

Ron wondered for a moment as he picked up Des' saddle, then grinned. "Stand-off's the place a bunch of whites stood off a thousand Indian braves in a battle of the Riel Rebellion," he explained. Walking over to his pinto, he tossed Des' saddle over his own. "Dad'll dig you up a cinch out of the Indian storehouse," he said. "What's your name?"

Des studied the sky and scratched his head. "Des Harmon," he answered absently. "I wanted to make Leavings tonight."

Ron shook his head as he surveyed Rocket.

"I wouldn't ride after dark with that prize as bait," he advised soberly. "You'd better stay all night with us."

Des thought of Lynn's words.

"Okay, if you're sure I won't be a nuisance," he agreed. Walking over to Rocket he took up his reins. "We'll make more distance tomorrow," he promised, then followed Ron down a trail along the bank of the rushing river.

"Sure," Ron said, leading the way. He turned as they came within sight of the Agency, a low rambling house along the riverbank. Camped on the hills around were a hundred-odd tepees. Smoke came from the tops of them. Indian squaws squatted before them cooking over smoldering campfires.

"The Indians are celebrating," Ron explained. "Joe Ghost-Chest is home on furlough with his medal. Tonight they'll have a big powwow and dance."

Des would gladly have missed all this and ridden on to Leavings if he dared. But he accepted the inevitable and, following Ron, came at length to the big red barn.

Across, beyond the Indian encampment, another man was preparing for the night, too. A lone rider who had trailed Des, had seen him follow Ron into the barn, then, wheeling his black horse, made his way stealthily down along the riverbank to a squat log cabin.

As he rode into the yard, a man came out of the cabin. A tall dark half-Indian with deep-set, black eyes.

"Hello, Mike," El Gato greeted him.

"You?" Mike said, without enthusiasm.

"Yes, me." El Gato smiled and dismounted. "I'm sleeping till midnight, then I'm riding on to Robber's Roost."

"Business?" Mike asked.

El Gato's eyes went back along the river to the top of the big red barn Des and Rocket had entered.

"*Si*," he said, at length. "Business with a crazy boy at Robber's Roost. He's got a horse I want."

Suddenly, he turned and tossed his black's reins to Mike. "Feed and water him," he said. "Then come up to the cabin. I'll want to eat."

Without another word, El Gato wheeled with catlike grace and moved toward Mike's cabin. As he walked he smiled, thinking how easy getting the Palomino from that kid would be. How simple, there at Robber's Roost, and in the dark.

CHAPTER VI

NIGHT CHASE

Meanwhile, Des bedded Rocket in the box stall next Ron's pinto, giving him a slim feed of oats and a rubdown. He was still worried about not making better progress—he couldn't have come more than thirty miles.

"But we'll make it up tomorrow, *amigo*." He slapped Rocket's sleek shoulder.

Rocket nickered softly and crowded close to Des.

Shouts from the Indian camp came through the door.

"Come on," Ron urged. "We'll have supper and then go up there."

Des was reluctant to leave Rocket.

"Quiet, *amigo*—you're okay here," he whispered to the big gold horse nibbling nervously at his hay.

Rocket seemed to settle down, then, and Des, with a last backward glance, followed Ron out of the barn. The box stall seemed tight enough. Rocket couldn't get out, and yet—

Des walked up the double row of cottonwoods to enter the two-story white house and meet Mrs. Stanley, a small woman with soft brown eyes and an olive skin. Like my mother, Des thought, as Ron said, "Mom, this is

Des Harmon. His cinch broke—he's staying all night."

"I should think you'd be afraid out here among all these Indians," Des said, without thinking. He couldn't get his mind off Rocket. He hoped supper would be ready soon.

Mrs. Stanley laughed, looking beyond Des and to his left.

"With Corporal Trenholm stationed down the river?" she asked.

Des swung around, flushing, his eyes popping at the smiling "Mountie" in scarlet coat, black whipcord riding pants with the three-inch yellow band running down into knee-length tan riding boots.

"Oh, I didn't know," he mumbled. But, someway, Trenholm's presence made leaving Rocket safer.

Mr. Stanley, a smallish bald man with twinkling blue eyes, put Des at his ease.

"Don't let my wife tease you," he said. Then he looked at Ron. "We'd better eat," he went on. "I can see Ron's anxious to get up with the Indians." He sat down at the head of the table.

"I'll have to show up, too," Corporal Trenholm said, taking a chair next Mrs. Stanley. "The Indians are pretty excited about Joe's medal—and rightly so."

Ron motioned Des into a chair beside him, as a black-eyed Indian girl came in silently on beaded moccasins bringing a huge platter of roast dried venison. Around it were baked potatoes and turnips.

Mr. Stanley began to serve.

"Ever see an Indian powwow?" Corporal Trenholm asked Des. He grinned. "I should say, hear one?"

Des checked himself just in time. He'd almost blurted, "No, and I'd rather not—I'd rather go out and keep an eye on Rocket." But the sight of Corporal Trenholm's tanned face and friendly gray eyes silenced him.

"No," he said, taking the plate Mr. Stanley served him, "and I'm sure looking forward to it—if my horse is okay. I don't know—all this excitement."

"He'll settle down," Trenholm assured Des.

Suddenly, above the sound of his voice, and the night wind in the cottonwoods, came the low chant of voices and the steady throb of drums.

"They're warming up," Ron exclaimed excitedly. "Come on, Des."

"Ron, finish your dinner," Mrs. Stanley said firmly.

Ron stuffed his venison down and Des followed his lead.

After five minutes, Des excused himself and followed the impatient Ron out into the darkness. His steps took him without thinking down to the stable. He almost ran as he drew near it.

Rocket whinnied as he approached and pranced in his

box stall, making the planks echo with his pounding hoofs.

Des opened the door to his stall, and going inside put his hand along Rocket's shoulder. It was quivering and wet with sweat.

"*Amigo—amigo,*" he soothed. Then he said to Ron, "I'd better stay here. Anyway, I must get an early start. I've missed Leavings tonight. I'll have to ride on to Robber's Roost tomorrow."

"That bunch of horse thieves?" Ron stared, his face for once becoming dead serious. "I don't know—I hear some funny things about that ranch."

Des had already made up his mind. He had to get on toward Lethbridge as fast as he could.

"We'll make it, okay, won't we, *amigo?*" he said, rubbing Rocket's quivering nose.

The pound of drums coming through the stable door brought Ron back with a jerk.

"Okay, Des," he said in a disappointed voice. "It's up to you." He led the way to a cot in a saddle room at the other end of the barn from Rocket's stall. "I'll call you in the morning." He turned and walked along the plank floor and on out the door, his footsteps fading on the gravel driveway.

Des loosed his bedroll from the saddle and rolled it

out on the cot. He listened a moment. Rocket seemed to have settled down.

He took off his windbreaker, slipped out of his high-heeled boots and crawled under the blanket, stretching out. He yawned, his eyelids heavy with sleep. The drums—their throbbing. He closed his eyes and suddenly slept.

Hours later, Des sat bolt upright in bed.

The high rhythmic chant of Indians pierced the still night. Firelight from distant fires danced on the room's single windowpane.

From Rocket's stall came the pounding of hoofs. Scream after scream of fright came from the horse, and his solid body could be heard thudding against the planks of the stall.

Des leaped from bed, groping madly for his boots.

"Amigo! Amigo!" he called, scooping up his lariat. "I'm coming!"

He made it to the door of the alley, between the stalls. But the crash of a splintering door filled his ears. Then the sound of hoofs.

He flung out into the alley, just in time to grab futilely for Rocket's hackamore rope and see his flowing silver tail disappear through the door and fade into the darkness.

Des ran bareheaded, his plaid shirt flying, following the direction of the peculiar sound of Rocket's pounding hoofs. Up past the Indian dances and on out to the sloping prairie.

"*Amigo, amigo!*" he called.

Corporal Trenholm overtook him on horseback and Des sprang up astride behind him.

"My horse," he explained against the flying wind. "I should have slept in his stall."

"He won't go far," Trenholm said. "The band of hobbled Indian mares will stop him."

Des shook his head.

"He's gone," he said. "But, I'll get him if it's the last thing I ever do."

He clasped Corporal Trenholm's waist and hung on.

They climbed the ground that sloped from the river bed, back two miles. Suddenly, Corporal Trenholm said, "Just as I thought—there's your horse, Des."

Des looking around Trenholm's scarlet coat caught a glimpse of his big gold horse standing off maybe a hundred feet. He had his head thrown up, staring at them.

Des slipped to the ground and walked across the soft green grass.

"*Amigo,*" he breathed, above the lump in his throat.

Rocket whinnied softly.

Des moved ahead, hardly daring to breathe. If Rocket should bolt—fade into the night with the boundless prairie ahead—

The Palomino tossed his great gold head, sending the hackamore rope over his back. Now there was nothing to hold him.

Des walked stolidly on, breathing, *"Amigo—amigo —wait—"*

Rocket whinnied again. He turned as if to run, then squared to Des and let him walk up to him.

"Amigo," Des whispered, his knees weak as water under him. "Don't ever do that again."

"Your rope," Trenholm reminded gently, ignoring the huskiness in Des' voice.

Des silently nodded and slipped his lariat over Rocket's flicking ears, then with one hand twined in his mane he sprang astride him.

Like two ghost riders, in the stark moonlight, they started off in the direction of the river and the dotted fires of the Indian camps.

"Might as well see the Sun Dance," Corporal Trenholm said, nodding toward a big campfire in the distance. "It'll be over in half an hour and I'll ride on down with you."

Des nodded, and they rode on to sit their horses on a knoll overlooking the dance.

Des saw four young Indian braves step into single file before the fire.

"Some war bonnets," he whispered, his eyes running along their big eagle-feathered headdresses.

The corporal nodded.

"That boy in the lead is Joe's brother. He's going into the army next week. Watch!"

Des nodded, fascinated by the swift rhythmical movement of the four dancers.

"Ah-ee— Ah-ee—!" they chanted, waving rattles in their left, and bows and arrows in their right hands. Weaving and hopping— Weaving and hopping—

"Ah-ee— Ah-ee—!" chanted the voices of Indians circled around them.

"Boy—some show," Des whispered, still uneasy, still wanting to get on down to the Agency and to bed. He had a long day before him tomorrow.

At last the dance was over.

The low guttural grunts of the braves mingled with the shrill cries of the squaws came to an end.

"That's all." Corporal Trenholm's grin was kindly. "Joe's properly made a hero among the Blood Indians and we can go to bed."

He reined his dark brown horse to the left and led Des down the trail toward the Agency.

Off to the right, on another knoll, a lone rider on a lithe black horse studied the boy on the big Palomino, then, with an evil grin, swung east.

"My young *amigo*," he breathed through white teeth. "We meet tomorrow night at Robber's Roost—where I settle accounts for that ducking and get your horse. *Si*?"

He put the spurs to his mare and, as Des faded into the darkness with Corporal Trenholm, rode swiftly over the ridge and toward Robber's Roost to wait for him.

CHAPTER VII

ROBBER'S ROOST

Des woke at the touch of Ron's hand on his shoulder.

"I ought to let you sleep till tomorrow morning," he said, ruefully. "Then Corporal Trenholm could go with you."

Des slipped out of his bedroll, dressed, and washed his face down at the river.

"I'll be okay—with Rocket," he said, coming back to walk in beside the big golden horse.

"You should be," Corporal Trenholm said, coming in beside Des. "James, the boss at Robber's Roost, and his gang are away some place. There's only a guard left at The Roost."

Des' heart turned a flop. So James, the guy who'd tried to capture Rocket, was the boss at Robber's Roost? He hid his concern by grabbing a currycomb and giving Rocket's golden coat a good grooming.

"That fellow—He's the worst of the lot—John Three-Persons. You better lay over, Des," Ron pleaded.

Des figured a minute. He wasn't anxious to tangle with any half-breed. But he'd only made thirty miles.

That left more than a hundred to do in three days—if he was to get to Lethbridge and have one day's rest before the stampede.

"I've got to mooch on, Ron," he said. With a final slap along Rocket's sleek flank, he tossed the currycomb in the rack beside the stall door. "There, *amigo*," he said. "Now for some oats, and breakfast, and then—"

In half an hour he'd eaten the breakfast of oatmeal, bacon and eggs, and hot cakes that bustling little Mrs. Stanley served him.

"Mr. Stanley said to tell you good-bye," she said, softly, pressing a brown parcel under his arm. "You'll make Leavings long before lunchtime, Des," she said. "Then, there's no place short of Fort Mackie."

"You mean Robber's Roost," Des said steadily. "That's my way."

Mrs. Stanley's eyes widened with concern. "The short cut. You mustn't, Des. The closest ranch to that thieves' hangout is Starrs'—Jim Starr, his wife, and daughter, Nina—but it's way downriver. Too far for protection."

Ron grinned. "Maybe if you hit the Starrs', you'll discover the Lost Mine—solid gold nuggets sticking out of the riverbank."

Mrs. Stanley's indignant eyes fell on Ron, then turned again to Des. "He's joking of course—there is no Lost Mine."

"Well, maybe Nina Starr'll draw his picture, then," Ron persisted. "She learned to do that before they moved from Mexico."

Des smiled at Ron, then tried to reassure Mrs. Stanley. He hated to appear obstinate, but going by Fort Mackie would bring him into Lethbridge the day of the stampede.

"I'll be okay," he said, then dug two dollars out of his levis. "I want to pay for last night," he said.

Mrs. Stanley's face expressed her indignation.

"I ought to spank you, Des Harmon," she said, a smile playing at her lips.

"But the cinch, and Rocket's oats, and all this food!" Des blurted, his face brick-red.

"Skip it," Ron exploded.

Des shoved a dollar in Ron's pocket.

Ron tried to give it back.

They scuffled around the kitchen till Mrs. Stanley made them quit. But when they did, the dollar was still with Ron.

"Okay for you—but I'll get even with you for this," Ron promised.

Des grinned and shook hands with Mrs. Stanley.

"Come down to the *Twin Anchor*, Ron," he said, then made for the door.

Down at the barn, he led Rocket out across the planks,

saddled him, tied the lunch inside his bedroll behind the cantle, then climbed into the saddle.

"So long, Ron," he said.

Ron made a last try.

"You don't know what you're riding into," he said, glumly. "That fellow's a bad egg. You might go to bed at night, okay. But in the morning be tied up like a pig —and *amigo*!" He kissed his fingers to the light morning breeze.

Des had made up his mind: getting to that stampede was the thing—and winning the prize money to buy Rocket.

"Take it easy, Ron," he said, and touching Rocket lightly with his spurs rode out of the barn and east.

Rocket, head held high, silver mane flying, paced out of the gate, along the river trail, then at Des' light rein on his neck, swung sharply toward two buttes on the morning skyline.

The sun shone brightly. Gophers whistled from their mounds. A hawk wheeled in the blue sky above them, and off to the left a slinking coyote stalked a white-faced calf frisking dangerously far from his mother.

Des rode steadily east, to the buttes, through Leavings, then dropped down the east slope toward a distant set of banks. He wondered about the Starrs, but rode steadily on.

Around three o'clock he passed the fork in the trail. To the left lay Fort Mackie, but it was twenty miles out of his way. To the right, lay Robber's Roost, there in the bend of the St. Marys.

He suddenly decided to try a little experiment.

"Tell you what, *amigo*," he said, riding Rocket back down the trail he'd come, a hundred yards. "I'll let you decide. I'll hang the reins on the horn. Ride you down the trail. You take the left fork, it's Fort Mackie; the right, we'll risk Robber's Roost."

He held his breath as the forked trail loomed ahead. He sat straight in the saddle, lest his body sway Rocket's choice.

Suddenly, Rocket reached the fork and, without a second's hesitation, swung sharply down the right trail.

"And Robber's Roost it is," Des whispered. "Come what may." In spite of himself, his heart bumped his ribs as he picked up the reins and sent Rocket straight toward the line of cutbanks miles ahead.

From the time Des rode Rocket into the yard of Robber's Roost, he wished he'd gone by Mackie. But it was too late to change his mind now. He'd promised Lynn not to ride at night, and already the sun had set in the west.

"How!" Three-Persons grunted his greeting from the cookhouse doorway. "You stay all night—"

"Sounds like an order," Des decided.

"Me alone—glad have you," Three-Persons added.

Des looked him square in his shifting black eyes.

"He's lying," he decided. With his heart pounding, Des studied the coming night. He could hardly see the corrals down the trail toward the river, and the log barn seemed just a blurr in the twilight. Well, he shrugged. He was in for it, and no use showing fear before this leering man with the broken teeth and the gash over his darting eyes.

"Okay—I'm glad, too," Des said, getting down.

"Me take horse to barn," Three-Persons said. With powerful hands he grasped Rocket's reins, and the next instant picked himself from the weeds and grass of the dooryard.

"He's wild—doesn't like strangers," Des hastened to explain. He didn't like the way Three-Persons' eyes glittered. It didn't match the smile he mustered for Des' benefit.

"You bringum?" the half-breed grunted.

He led the way down to the log barn, showed Des where to water Rocket, showed him the stall and where to hang his saddle.

"You sleep in bunkhouse," the man grunted, refusing to meet Des' eyes. "Along with me."

Des didn't argue, but he made up his mind that, when bedtime came, he'd sleep in the oatbin just off Rocket's stall. Just now, Rocket was having a fit.

"Easy, *amigo*," Des said, going in beside him, pulling his head down.

Rocket was trembling, his black ears lying close to his head.

Des got a currycomb and put in twenty minutes grooming his coat. Then, he washed his back free of sweat-grime brought there by the saddle blanket. After this, he took a can and opened the door leading to the oatbin. It was a tiny room with a single window—a pile of oats on one side and a cot by the door.

"Oats free, take plenty," Three-Persons said gruffly.

Des' hand tightened on the gallon can. Something was wrong here. Filling the can, he walked by Three-Persons to dump the oats into Rocket's feedbox.

Rocket refused them!

Des put his hand along Rocket's neck. The big horse was shaking like a leaf. Des gulped, and had hard work to keep from jumping as Three-Persons said, "Now—we eat."

Des hesitated, then forced himself to follow the broad back of the breed back to the log cookhouse.

Three-Persons stood aside to let Des enter.

Feeling the hairs rise on his neck, Des walked stiffly through the door.

The half-breed followed, banging the door. And as he did, Des was sure he heard another door close.

Walking to the window, his beating heart all but suffocating him, Des looked out into the gathering night and saw a granary door banging in the wind.

"Ghost!" The man grinned beside him.

Des wheeled, and for the first time, saw how powerfully Three-Persons was built. The stealthy power in his frame as he moved on beaded moccasins to fry the inevitable eggs and bacon and put them before Des.

"Grub free—eat plenty," he grunted.

Des slid his lariat up along his arm. He never moved without having it with him. Then, taking up his fork, he started to eat.

"The condemned ate a hearty supper," he breathed.

Three-Persons' ears picked it up.

"That good joke." He grinned slyly. Then, with a sudden shift of mood, added, "that good horse you ride, too."

Des nodded.

The half-breed shot Des a calculating stare.

"Kid like you and horse like that should have Mountie ride along, too."

Des felt the keen eyes searching him out. And, as he hesitated, Des would have bet a cow that another pair of ears listened for his reply.

At length, he said, casually, "Maybe Corporal Trenholm did ride with me, today."

Three-Persons grinned, and shook his big bearlike head.

"You lie," he grunted. "Corporal Trenholm at Standoff. Come tomorrow."

Des forced himself to go on eating. Slowly, quietly, in spite of his racing heart, lifting his fork up and down, up and down.

He could have sworn he heard footsteps, now close, now fading into the darkness. But he went on eating.

Three-Persons seemed to be listening for something, too.

Suddenly, as Des finished his plate of bacon and eggs, the pounding of hoofs reached him—coming from the barn. Then Rocket's shrill scream of fright.

Des sprang to his feet as the man lunged for him.

Des slipped to one side, and quick as a flash, formed a loop in his rope. As the Indian lunged past him, Des deftly dropped the loop. The moccasined feet stepped in it and Des jerked with all his might.

The big man went down, his head hitting the stove edge as he fell.

Without losing a moment, Des flipped his rope loose from the unconscious man and coiled it.

"No need to tie you up," he whispered, then leaped for the door and let himself into the night.

From behind him came the opening of another door. A dark shadow moved around the house toward the kitchen—a lithe shadow that Des recognized.

"El Gato," he whispered. "And he didn't see me get out."

Des ran softly down the trail to the barn. He flung the door open and raced inside.

"*Amigo,*" he whispered to Rocket's nickering response. "We have to move, fast."

Rocket quieted down. He stood while Des flung his saddle on, tightened the cinch.

Des strained his ears for footsteps.

They came, as he knew they must.

Des felt his knees turn to water.

There wasn't time to bridle Rocket. He led him from the stall, down the plank center between the stalls to the back door. It led to a high pole corral.

Already, in the front door, loomed the lithe shadowy figure of El Gato.

Des sprang into the saddle.

"Stop!" El Gato yelled. "I shoot!"

Des measured the corral fence—six feet high, with

only a fifty-foot run. He moved his hand down along Rocket's neck.

"*Amigo,*" he breathed. "It is now—or never."

Rocket raced for the pole fence, gathered himself, and leaped into the air, seemed to hang like a great golden statue in the dark, then went over.

Des yelled in triumph.

A shot rang out.

Des felt a gentle nudge along his leather jumper sleeve and a slight jar on his saddle. Looking down, as Rocket raced on, he saw a bullet had plowed into the cantle of his saddle.

Leaning low along Rocket's neck, he urged him on.

"Come on, *amigo*," he breathed.

Another shot rang out. And another, but the great horse carried Des on.

They faded into the night with the sound of El Gato's voice like the scream of a cat, threatening, "I get you yet, kid. You and that gold devil!"

CHAPTER VIII

THE LOST MINE

KEEPING FAR ENOUGH BACK FROM THE RIVERBANK TO miss the wash-coulees running into the main river, and sighting by the two end stars of the Big Dipper, Des pressed Rocket north and east toward Lethbridge.

He rode fast, straining his ears for the sound of El Gato's pursuit.

"Come on, *amigo*," he whispered, running his hand along Rocket's sweaty neck. El Gato would make another try for Rocket.

And Rocket, with his fighting heart, stretched out into a tireless pace that carried Des on and on.

But as hour after hour passed, with the steady beat of Rocket's hoofs on the prairie grass, Des found his anxiety lessening, and his eyelids drooping.

He yawned, and shivered. "Cold!"

Did he imagine it, or was that a pale line in the east?

Rocket dipped through a swale, then slackened by a buckbrush clump. And, when Des didn't urge him on, suddenly dropped his head and, unsuccessfully because of the bit, tried to graze.

Des grinned sleepily down at the knee-high clump of bushes.

"A bedroom—what do you know?" he whispered and yawned again.

In a moment, he was off Rocket, had him unsaddled and picketed on the length of lariat. Then unrolling his bedroll, Des crawled inside, stretched out, yawned again, and closed his eyes.

When Des awakened, it was daylight, with the sun beating down on his face. He could hear the steady sound of tearing grass—Rocket getting breakfast.

Des sat up, hungrily staring around.

"Boy, wish I was a horse—hey!" He jumped up, then grinned foolishly, looking down at a fuzzy red and white Hereford calf left there for the day by its mother.

Des, just for fun, tried to get the calf to jump and run.

"Smart guy," he said, when the calf wouldn't budge. "This way, the coyotes won't get you."

Des took hold of Rocket's picket rope and pulled him to his side.

"Well, boy," he said, grinning, "Seems to me I smell bacon cooking—maybe Jim Starr's bacon. Coming right up from those gold-studded riverbanks of Lost Mine."

Rocket nuzzled his windbreaker, while Des, still wondering why Jim Starr had ever left Mexico, examined El Gato's bullet hole in the tree of his saddle.

"Close call," he said.

Rocket shook his head.

"Oh!" Des eyed him. "You don't think so?"

Des took some grass and scrubbed Rocket's back, slapped the folded blanket on it, then the saddle.

In less than five minutes, he rode on, north and east, following the course of the St. Marys. And suddenly, he came to a bluff on the river where, out from a little projection high above the winding stream, a black crow with white wings flew, croaking and wheeling above Des.

"Git out—!" it screeched. "Git out—!"

Des rubbed his eyes.

"I guess I am pretty hungry—but am I delirious?"

"Git out! Git out! Help, murder! Murder!" screeched the crow.

"A tame crow with a slit tongue," Des decided.

Suddenly, the crow wheeled for a last screaming assault at Des, then dived down the bank and across the river toward a little cabin where smoke poured from a tin chimney.

"Breakfast," Des whispered, licking his lips. "And oats for you, *amigo*—that's for us."

Touching Rocket lightly with his spurs, Des rode along the St. Marys' banks for maybe another half mile, picked his way down to the swirling water's edge, then plunged in. Holding his legs across the horn of his saddle, Des rode the swimming horse across, climbed the sharp bank and stood until Rocket got his wind.

For a moment, he had time to study the peculiar vein of clay running along a cutbank upstream.

"Looks like Lost Mine Vein, *amigo*," he said, slapping Rocket's wet, glistening neck. "Or hadn't you heard," he kidded, "about the two men who came to Lethbridge with a pint jar full of nuggets?"

He took up Rocket's reins to go on toward the cabin nestling in a grove of cottonwoods about a quarter of a mile upriver. Maybe this was Starr's ranch?

"Please hold it. He's so beautiful. All wet and golden with the sun on him," a clear voice said. "No, don't turn your head."

Des sat straight, looking ahead, till suddenly the voice said, "Now—I can fill it in at home."

Des swung around to see a redheaded tomboyish girl in levis, and knew that she was Nina Starr.

"What's that?" he asked, nodding toward the paper pad in her freckled hand.

"Your horse," she said, then laughed at Des' disappointed face. "You, too, silly."

"Let's see," Des said, getting off Rocket and walking toward her.

She shook her head till her dark-red hair danced on her slim shoulders.

"It's no good," she said, thrusting the picture behind her. "Might be if Dad could find Lost Mine—and send me to Calgary Art School." She smiled wistfully. "But he can't do it on a bunch of range dogies."

Des managed, as they walked toward the cabin, to see what she'd sketched.

Boy—that was Rocket, all right. And that slim dark kid he guessed was himself—though he figured he looked a lot different from that.

They reached the yard and walked around to the kitchen door.

A slim dark woman with a soft voice came out.

"Mother, this is—?" Nina broke off, then flushed.

"Des Harmon," Des said laughing. "And this is my horse, Rocket."

"Wonderful," Mrs. Starr said, staring at Rocket, who was rubbing his ears against Des' leather jacket. "I'm Mrs. Starr, and this is Nina."

"I know," Des said. "Mrs. Stanley told me."

"Ron, too, I suppose," Nina tartly added.

"Nina," Mrs. Starr cautioned.

"Well, he said something about the mine," Des grinned.

Suddenly their talk was interrupted by a screeching voice coming around the corner.

"I'm Screamer," it said.

Then the voice appeared. Jim Starr, slim and boyish in his ten-gallon hat, hove into sight with a black crow perched on his shoulder. Starr's lean face still bore the burned old-leather hue of his years in Mexico.

"Git out! Git out! Help, murder!" screeched the crow.

Starr grinned at Des, then reached for Rocket's reins.

Rocket didn't mind—seemed in fact to know him.

"Come along, I'll feed your horse," Starr said. "And tell you about Screamer."

They walked down to the log barn, with Des telling Starr his name, and where he was going.

Starr nodded, then reached a sunburned hand to stroke Screamer's black feathers.

"This modest bird came with the ranch," he explained with a laugh, then sobered. "He was here when I came up from Dorado, Mexico, to homestead this shebang."

"Lost Mine and all," Nina, who'd come with them, put in with a rueful smile.

"The one Ron told me about?" Des smiled back.

Frowning at Nina, Starr nodded. "Those two men who originally discovered Lost Mine—if there ever was one—are buried downriver about a mile. When I got here all that was left was the old cabin and this screaming crow flying along the river."

"And you never found a trace of the nugget vein?" Des asked, staring at Nina's wistful face.

"Nope—and I've given up trying," Starr said. "I'll throw Rocket, here, his oats, then we'll go back to breakfast."

Going up to the cabin, and all through breakfast, the sight of Nina's face bothered Des. He couldn't forget what art school would do for her. And Jim Starr, sitting there at the head of the table, lapsed into moody silence.

Des could tell they were all hard up. Really hard up.

A rider came up the trail.

Des saw Jim Starr's eyes meet Mrs.. Starr's. Then he saw the relief in both as the rider went on without coming in.

"The sheriff," Nina told Des later out in the yard. "Dad's about to lose this place to the bank. We came up from Mexico two years ago. Last year we had a poor calf crop. And this last winter the cold killed off some of his best cows."

They wandered up along the river. The cliffs had a secret forbidding look as they walked along. Des studied them grimly. Nina's harassed eyes tormented him.

"Didn't your father ever find even a trace of that vein?" he asked. "What about Screamer? Didn't he help?"

"No—Dad tried to get Screamer to fly along the banks. But the crow only perched on his shoulder, screeching, " 'Git out, help, murder!' "

Des nodded, and followed the banks upstream. For nearly an hour, he sweated along, leaving Nina far behind, kicking clods of dirt from likely-looking spots, peering sharply into cracks in the bank's vertical height.

Once, on a sandbank at the edge of the swirling water, he thought he'd found something—a dull yellow glowing up at him. His heart bumped, as he stooped over. Then a foolish grin spread over his face as his fingers riffled through the worthless sand.

"Fool's gold," he quoted from what he'd learned in chemistry. "Iron pyrites."

Des gave up then, too. Anxiously, he scanned the sun in the sky. His watch had stopped, but it must be ten o'clock and he still had thirty miles to cover that day.

He walked back along the river to find Nina sitting on a rock, her hand trailing in the water, minnows nibbling at her fingers.

"Phew!" Des sat down beside her. "Guess I'll have to give up."

Nina nodded, gently. "Like Dad. He just went back to raising cows, and Screamer went back to living in the house daytimes and lighting out at night. No telling where he goes, or where he perches. Maybe he's got a nugget-nest some place—"

Des suddenly stared at Nina, and a bell seemed to ring within him.

"Say that again, Nina," he demanded.

Slowly, she repeated her words.

Easy, then, careful not to let on—for it would be cruel to Nina if it didn't pan out—Des guided the way back to the cabin.

"Is Mr. Starr still here?" he asked, his heart thudding his ribs. He'd need help.

"He rode west—but you can catch him," Mrs. Starr said. "Why did you want him?"

Des' heart sank. If he couldn't get Jim Starr? He raced to the barn and getting Rocket out mounted him. Then, his eyes searching far ahead, put the big golden horse in pursuit of Jim Starr.

Two miles upriver, Des overtook him.

Jim raised tired questioning eyes as Des rode up. And Des couldn't help picturing how crazy it would look to Starr if what he had in mind didn't work out. But Nina's eyes forced him to go on. Taking a deep breath and grasping the tree of his saddle, he said, "Mr. Starr, I have an idea, and I'll need help to carry it out."

Jim Starr took off his hat, and with maddening slowness stared west.

"Well, I don't know. I've got to get a couple of strays —and it'll take me all my time, today."

Des knew that if what he had in mind worked out, a couple of stray dogies more or less wouldn't matter to Starr.

"It won't take long," he urged. "Fact is, coming along the river this morning, I spotted something I want."

"On my land?" Jim asked.

Des gulped. He hadn't thought of that. With his heart beating fast, he pointed downriver to the point from which the crow had flown.

"That your bluff?" he asked softly, his mouth dry with excitement.

"Yep—"

"Then, let's go."

He answered the questions in Starr's eyes by giving orders.

"We'll need another rope."

"Anything else?" Jim Starr's curiosity was being aroused.

Des shook his head and led the way by the barn to pick up the rope, then on down to the ford. He shoved

Rocket into the water, looking back at Jim's bay cayuse.

Once across the river, it was the work of minutes to reach the cutbank.

Des loosed his lariat and fastened one end around his waist, then looked over the edge of the precipice.

Jim Starr balked.

"No, sir. No boy's going to get killed and me help him."

Des could hardly wait to see what was in Screamer's nest on that ledge just under the precipice edge.

"It's easy," he said, dismounting and motioning Starr to change horses. "Get on Rocket, here, and take your dallies."

Jim Starr finally gave in, joining the two ropes.

Des studied a moment, then walked over to Rocket, trailing the rope as he walked.

"*Amigo,*" he whispered, bringing the big golden head down to his, and motioning to Starr. "Let him get on, quiet—"

Rocket stood while Starr mounted him, then with Des leading him, came to within ten feet of the cutbank's edge.

"Okay, I'm going over," he said. "One jerk, pay out more rope. Two, pull up."

He sat down on the edge and swung his legs over the bank. The rush of the river, like a clear blue thread, came clearly up to him. And he felt the soft upsweep of wind on the cliff.

"Okay." He tautened the line. Then, holding his breath, he swung into space.

Down. Down. Down. Ten feet, fifteen—

There was the nest, a round jumble of twigs on a point. It looked pretty small to Des.

And here came old Screamer, flapping around his head, croaking, "Get out! Get out! Help, thief! Help, thief!"

Des felt the rope tremble. He caught his breath, and looked down the dizzy cliff. But he breathed deeply and trusted Rocket.

He jiggled the rope once. He dropped another five feet, and his hand could reach out and touch the nest!

"Empty!" The word slipped from Des' taut lips. "Just clayed sticks with mud in the bottom."

For a second, hanging there, Des stared dully at the nest. The picture he had was of Jim Starr, forced to move on, to give up his ranch, and Nina missing school. It wasn't pleasant.

Then, as the sun came out from behind a cloud, something dull yellow caught Des' eyes. He reached forward, and with Screamer's wings flapping in his face, gathered the weighty nest to him and gave two short jerks to the rope.

Back beside Rocket, Des handed the nest over to Jim Starr, who was just dismounting.

"Nuggets," he said. "From your Lost Mine."

"Nuggets," Jim repeated, mechanically, his hands searching unbelievingly among them. Then his voice sparkled. "For Nina. For the ranch, and Mother!"

Des turned gently, coiling up his rope. Boy, did he feel glad? And he guessed he'd have to roll, for Lethbridge was still far away and El Gato must be still behind him.

CHAPTER IX

BOMBED

But Jim Starr had some ideas on Des' pulling out.

"Oh no, Des," he said, carefully picking the nuggets from Screamer's nest and wrapping them in his red bandanna. "We'll take these down to the ranch—celebrate today. Tomorrow, when you do go, half of these nuggets go with you. And with me as a bodyguard."

Des couldn't help being tempted by Starr's offer. It would be a funny Mexican—even a wealthy one like Señor Reyes—who wouldn't jump at a thousand pesos for Rocket. But Des shook his head and began tying his coiled rope on the horn of his saddle.

"Skip it," he said, picking up Rocket's reins and climbing into his saddle. "And tell Nina and Mrs. Starr goodbye." He grinned at Screamer circling his head and screeching. "Git out! Git out!" Then he turned back to Jim. "Another thing, you might teach that bird some manners for the next time I come."

With a touch of his spurs on Rocket's sleek flanks, and with Jim Starr still protesting, Des rode north and east into the sea of green prairie ahead.

Starr caught up with him, his face filled with concern. "I'd go now," he blurted. "But, I must get to that bank at Leavings—I'm obliged to, today."

Des didn't slacken his pace. Every minute was precious, when he didn't know where El Gato was.

"I know, and I'll be okay," he said. "Well, so long."

Jim Starr dropped back, and Des rode on. In ten minutes he'd topped a rise and, dropping to the other side, put Jim Starr from sight.

Riding along, Des felt a mounting concern. He'd killed far too much time. It was after noon; he'd never make it to Stanley before dark—and he'd had enough of night riding.

He checked Rocket at a fork in the trail. His sense of direction told him that Stanley lay over there—and this trail led that way. Why not take another short cut? It might throw El Gato off his trail.

As he sat Rocket's back, considering, a silver bomber from Lethbridge air base droned over, high in the cloudless sky.

Rocket shied, and began to buck from panic.

"Whoa, Rocket! Whoa!" Des fought with the frantic horse trying to get clear of the plane's noise.

By the time Rocket was quiet, Des realized that he was well down the cut-off trail.

"Okay, *amigo*," he shrugged. "The cut-off trail it is."

He loosened Rocket's reins and gently shoved the lathered horse to his best ground-eating pace.

Hour after hour passed, with the ground fading under Rocket's piston-like legs. A coyote, scenting that Des had no gun, followed him, doglike, for what must have been two hours.

"Okay, guy," Des called, when once the slinking tan marauder drew close. "If you weren't such a chicken-stealer, I'd ask you on home."

"Yipeeee-ooooo-ooooo!" wailed the coyote.

Another plane, a mere dot in the sky, droned by.

"Getting used to 'em, Rocket," Des started to say—when, off to the left, the prairie seemed to explode, tossing sod high into the air. A dull *whoosh!* came to Des' ringing ears, and the concussion all but knocked him from the saddle.

Rocket swayed, then caught himself, and again started to buck.

"The bombing field!" burst from Des' lips. He hadn't seen any signs, but they'd blundered onto the restricted area—the Lethbridge practice-bombing range.

Des put the spurs to Rocket, straightening the bucking horse out, and putting him at a right-angled run from the plane.

But three more bombers in formation appeared out of

nowhere. Flying high. Too high, Des knew, for them to notice Rocket, whose coat was so like the color of the grass.

"They can't see us, *amigo*," he yelled, leaning into the saddle and giving Rocket his head. "We're in for—"

Whoosh—boom! Off to the left, a bomb hit the ground. *Whoosh—boom*—! *Whoosh—boom*—! Two bombs exploded to the right. The chain of death reached for Des and the flying horse.

Des braced himself. One more bomb on the string and it would be a direct hit. He flung Rocket to the right.

Whoosh—boom—! *Whoosh—boom*—! Another bomber had sent Bombs Away—!

Des reined Rocket to the left.

Whoosh—boom—! *Whoosh—boom*—! Two bombs exploded directly ahead of them.

Des gave up, then. They were bracketed. He was sunk. And it was a funny way to pass out—bombed to death in a peaceful country, on a peaceful day in June.

He braced himself for the next rack of bombs, lying low along the sweat-drenched neck of the terrified racing Rocket.

But no bombs came.

The third bombardier evidently hadn't pressed his release in rhythm. They'd come.

Des raced on, feeling terror crawl up his spine.

But still no more bombs came.

Des began to hope—when suddenly six more bombers appeared from the north. And with the neatness of stringing beads, laid down a pattern of destruction that would leave no bit of ground unbombed.

Des pulled up Rocket—spent from terror.

Whoosh—boom—! Whoosh—boom—!

A series of craters formed along his left.

Des clung to Rocket against the explosions.

Whoosh—boom—! Whoosh—boom—!

Off to his right a like pattern of death tore up the sod, sending it high into the dusty air.

Des steered Rocket for a bombed area.

"They don't duplicate," he yelled, encouraging his frantic horse.

But a third chain of bombs cut him off, rocking him in the saddle, and sending Rocket reeling.

Des crouched low, pulling Rocket to a blowing halt. He leaned down along his sweaty neck and sobbed, "This is it, *amigo!*"

Another half-sob escaped his lips, as he felt in that instant that they were through.

But suddenly, a peace settled over the flat prairie. And the dust, drifting away on a stiff breeze, took the planes with it.

Des got off Rocket, his knees weak, his eyes fixed on

a sign directly ahead: "Limit bombing range—no tres-
passing."

"The limit is right," he burst out. "And I'm it, riding
right across it."

He got on Rocket and pushed him hard north and
east against time, against the sun settling in a blood-red
western sky.

At nightfall, he sighted the flat white one-story patch
of buildings that must be Stanley.

In half an hour, sweat-drenched, and astride Rocket,
whose shoulders and flanks were also streaked with
sweat, Des rode down the single main street of the town
and pulled up in front of a shabby white two-story building with a sign reading, *Royal Hotel*.

Before he could throw a leg over his saddle, two men
came out of the battered door.

One, a lean, smiling man with a swarthy face and a
big silver-decorated sombrero—El Gato. Behind him,
stiff, his face expressing concern for Des, but doing his
duty, marched Corporal Trenholm.

Des' heart contracted. Here was trouble, or his name
wasn't Des Harmon.

CHAPTER X

EL GATO CLAWS DEEP

EL GATO CAME FORWARD TO STAND GRINNING UP AT DES.

"Ah, my friend, we have been waiting an hour—two hours— But now you are here with my horse. Yes?" He shrugged, and looked possessively at the big golden horse.

Des, his heart pounding, dismounted. Rocket stood, tired, sweaty, rolling his bit in his thirsty mouth.

"Your horse?" He glanced quickly at Corporal Trenholm. "How do you figure?" To hide his panic, he rubbed Rocket's left ear and whispered, "Okay, *amigo,* we'll get water and oats in a minute."

"This way I figure," El Gato said, softly. Turning to Corporal Trenholm, he purred, "You are witness I have not seen his horse—I cannot see under his mane—yet I will tell you that he is branded there."

Des felt the ground rocking under him. Was he going to lose Rocket to this Mexican—not be able to take him home?

"He's bluffing," he told the corporal, then turned to face El Gato. "Okay, what's he branded with?"

The Mexican slowly shrugged again.

100

"For one who put that brand there when this horse was a colt, that is easy," he said.

"Well, what is it?" snapped Trenholm.

"It is sombrero—like this." El Gato knelt, and with a sharp forefinger traced a sloping sombrero in the dirt.

Des steadied himself with Rocket's reins. The horse put his nose up against Des' leather jumper, gently nibbling the second from the top button.

"Easy, *amigo*," Des whispered.

He tried to trap El Gato, knowing about the vent bar under the sombrero brand.

"So, he is branded under the mane on this right side with the sombrero?" He turned to Corporal Trenholm. "If that is so, then Rocket is his."

Trenholm stepped forward.

"That right, El Gato?"

El Gato smiled tolerantly at Des.

"You are smart boy," he said. "But not smart enough. No." He turned to Trenholm. "There is more brand— a vent bar—which I also put on when I take the colt in payment for wages Señor Reyes owe me."

Trenholm faced Des kindly, but he had to be just.

"That right, Des?" His big tanned face showed how much he hated the job ahead.

Des took his time, his eyes boring into El Gato's, which tried to hold, wavered, then dropped. So, El Gato was really lying? Not about the brand—but some other way.

"Suppose it is?" Des demanded.

He swung on El Gato. "All right, suppose the sombrero is there and the vent. If Rocket is yours, where's your brand—why isn't Rocket branded with your iron?"

El Gato's smile widened.

"That is easy," he shrugged. "This colt was plenty tough. The second time I rope him—it is in the little round corral on the banks of the Rio Grande—I burn the vent on, then, before I can get my iron which is the box, this devil-colt kick all the ropes off, jump to his feet, leap the six-foot corral fence and disappear."

Des felt Rocket's nose against his back. He turned and the desire to keep Rocket burned within him like a flame.

"You must have had quite a life, *amigo*," he whispered. "Fighting blizzards and wolves. Shifting for yourself. You've earned something better."

Turning back to El Gato and the corporal, he fought for time. Huskily, he said, "This horse is played out. He's got to have feed and water no matter who owns him." With a quick step, he tried to lead Rocket around El Gato and toward a red barn behind the hotel.

El Gato blocked his path, putting a slim hand on Des' shoulder. "I ride on, tonight," he said.

At the touch of his hand, and the cruel look in his eyes, Des knew El Gato for the crook he was.

"You may ride on, El Gato, he heard his voice say, coolly. "But not on Rocket—now or ever."

"So?" El Gato's black eyes narrowed.

Trenholm stepped in, his sunburned face a study.

"His story sounds pretty straight, Des."

"But, I've written Señor Reyes," Des argued, the instinct of any good horseman pushing him toward feed and water for Rocket, with Trenholm and El Gato following. "He'll prove what I say—what El Gato says. For he must have been there at the time of the vent."

"By law, he had to be," Trenholm said.

Des stopped at a big round wooden horse trough about two feet high and ten feet in diameter. Slipping Rocket's bridle off, he watched the big golden horse bury his nose in the water, drinking greedily.

Des walked over to the pump and with a few brisk strokes brought water into a dipper which had hung beside it. Drinking, and watching El Gato over its edge, he knew that El Gato had been lying. But how to prove it? How to hang onto Rocket till the truth should come out?

"Boy!" He hung the dipper back on its hook, and wiped his mouth on the back of his leather sleeve. "That was very good."

Reaching Rocket, he turned to face El Gato.

"Let's wait and get Señor Reyes' side of this at Lethbridge?" he suggested. Suddenly, with El Gato's silence, Des felt better. He led Rocket toward the barn with El Gato by his side.

"I'm trying for the calf roping in the stampede," he said. "Five hundred dollars—it will be yours for Rocket if he is really yours."

El Gato smiled tolerantly as Des flung the barn door back and led Rocket into an empty stall.

"That is funny," he said, "for that prize is surely mine already—now that I will ride the big golden horse to win it." He walked back into the barn and brought out his own saddle trimmed with raw silver—the horn big and flat in Mexican style.

Des, who had unsaddled Rocket, was hanging his own saddle on a peg back of the horse. He did not step aside as El Gato advanced to resaddle the stallion.

He turned to Trenholm.

"It's his word against mine," he said.

Corporal Trenholm shook his head, regretfully.

"I'm sorry, Des. But it looks like he's got the goods on you."

Des didn't think so till El Gato dropped his saddle there on the plank barn floor and brought out a letter for Corporal Trenholm to read. And then, even with Trenholm reading, by the flickering light of a lantern hanging from the ceiling, that El Gato was the real owner of Rocket—that Señor Reyes said so—Des still didn't believe. He took the letter from Corporal Trenholm's hands and studied it. Then raised level eyes to stare El Gato down.

"It's a forgery," he said, flatly, handing the letter back to El Gato.

"So?" El Gato stepped menacingly to Des' side. "You deny the paper? That this is Señor Reyes writing? That this picture on the top is not the hacienda of Señor Reyes on the Rio de Sonora?"

Des, his heart thumping his ribs, nodded stoutly.

"You said it, El Gato," he said, softly.

"You think I do not own this horse?" El Gato's slim brown hand waved grandiloquently toward Rocket, munching his oats, his great tail gently lashing his powerful flanks.

Des held his breath. Corporal Trenholm's face told him that he was going to let El Gato have Rocket, much as he hated to.

A dog howled in the distance, lonesome and alone. Des wished he'd quit—it sounded too much like Rover at the *Twin Anchor,* the place he'd have to be very soon, and without Rocket.

Then Corporal Trenholm nodded.

"I'm sorry, Des. The letter looks okay, and El Gato's story sounds on the level."

"And he gets Rocket?"

El Gato read Trenholm's silence as consent. Showing white teeth in a triumphant grin, he grabbed up his saddle, jabbering, as he did so, to the police officer.

"*Gracias*, Señor," he babbled, moving in cautiously toward Rocket. "If you should ever come south of the Rio de Sonora—"

Des, watching, felt his heart bump against his ribs.

"*Amigo*," he whispered, excitement welling within him, for Rocket snorted at the approach of the Mexican. He jumped ahead in his stall, bringing his big golden body as far up between the planks as possible.

At El Gato's touch on his rump, he trembled, and, with a scream, doubled up his legs.

"*Sacre!*" El Gato's lithe body fell back just one inch ahead of those plunging hoofs.

El Gato tried going up by Rocket's head.

The great horse laid back his ears and bared his long teeth.

"*Amigo*," Des whispered, his eyes meeting the slow, amused, smiling ones of Corporal Trenholm.

El Gato climbed up into the haymow and slowly let his body down into Rocket's manger.

Rocket reared back, then forward, his forefeet pounding at the plank manger, coming nearer with each lunge to El Gato where he crouched in the hay.

Des came to El Gato's rescue, walking in beside Rocket. Soothing him, he let the frightened Mexican crawl from the manger, snarling, to safety.

"I kill him!" El Gato snarled, unsheathing a long knife.

"Oh, no!" Trenholm stepped in to take the knife from him. "Take him—if you can."

El Gato switched from anger to fawning. He turned to Des.

"You will take him to Lethbridge, then?"

Des studied the cunning face before him.

Bluntly he said. "Yes, to Lethbridge—to ride in the calf roping."

El Gato seemed to protest, then give in.

"It's only fair," Corporal Trenholm reminded. "Des rides him for the contest, then Señor Reyes will be there to prove ownership."

El Gato nodded, but his eyes didn't deceive Des.

"Señor Reyes decides." El Gato nodded.

Des, glad of the reprieve, went in to make sure of the knot on Rocket's hackamore. Then, in company with

Corporal Trenholm, he walked out over the sill of the barn, pulling the door closed.

El Gato, ahead of them, walked off in the direction of a big unpainted building with a high false front. Lights glowed from the windows. The sound of a juke-box came through the opened door.

"Tomorrow we ride for Lethbridge," he tossed back. "*Adios, señores.*"

Des followed Trenholm into the hotel, washed his sweat-grimed face and sat down at one of the two tables in the gaily wallpapered dining room.

Corporal Trenholm, very straight, very dignified, sat opposite. But he grinned at Des. "Boy, I'm hungry," he said.

A waitress in a plaid dress came in with bowls of vegetable soup.

"Ah!" Des broke crackers into his, and took up his spoon. "I wouldn't trust that El Gato as far as I can see in the dark," he said, sipping thoughtfully.

Trenholm nodded, and nothing further was said throughout the meal.

Afterward, Des climbed the stairs, and undressing got into the big white-iron bed. Lying there, he began think-ing of Rocket. Getting up, he slipped on his levis and shirt and went back out to the barn.

"*Amigo,*" he whispered, throwing back the big red door.

Rocket nickered sleepily, and Des shut the door again and started back to bed. Well, he was sure, now.

Going by the horse trough, the moon caught the clear clean water. Des couldn't resist it. He slipped off his shirt and levis and sank blissfully into the tank.

Going under, then up, and under again, blowing, tossing his dark hair out of his eyes, Des delighted in the cool, refreshing water on his body.

He plunged again, and again.

But suddenly, when he would have come up, Des felt a hand grasp his hair and bear down. Squirming over, Des stared up through a foot of water into the black murderous eyes of El Gato.

CHAPTER XI

ROCKET'S MYSTERY OWNER

In sudden panic, Des gulped water. Then, with the pressure of El Gato's hand increasing, he shot his legs against the side of the tank and, with a quick lunge down and under, plunged the Mexican in beside him.

"*Sacre!*" El Gato came up sputtering beside the naked Des, coughing, wiping the water from his black eyes.

Des made for the edge of the tank and over the side. He picked up his shirt and flung it over his dripping head.

A window from the hotel shot up and Corporal Trenholm leaned out.

"What's coming off out there?" he called softly.

Des, managing to get his head through his shirt, gave a quick glance at El Gato, his black suit sopping, the scarlet scarf around his thin neck a limp rag.

"Nothing," he called. "I'm just taking a bath in the horse trough."

"Oh!" Trenholm chuckled with relief. "Well, tell the rest of the buffalo good night, and come on to bed."

Des slipped into his levis and made for the hotel.

"Coming?" He turned at the hotel door and watched

the drenched El Gato, his sombrero on his sopping black hair, slink off into the dark. Then, breathing deep and tingling with the feel of cleanliness over him, he ran up the stairs and, removing his levis and shirt, jumped into bed.

"A bed—with sheets." Pretty good after so many nights in his bedroll. Des stretched out and yawned. He felt fine. And tomorrow Corporal Trenholm would ride to Lethbridge with him. He would have one day to rest, then, "*Amigo*," he whispered to his pillow, snuggling down into it, "the calf roping—" He slipped deeper under the covers—

Corporal Trenholm's hand on his shoulder awakened Des. He sat up, sleepily staring at the corporal's tunic.

"Dressed?" he said. "And it's just getting light."

Trenholm nodded, gravely, staring out the east window to the streak of light on the horizon.

"I've got to go back to Broken Arrow," he explained. Des thought a moment.

"James rounded in too many horses, I suppose—got some ranchers' stuff?"

The corporal nodded again.

"That's right—there's trouble. A night rider just came in and gave me the message." His eyes fell with concern on Des. "Now you'll have to go on alone."

Des considered. There was still El Gato. And Señor Reyes. He slipped from bed and dressed quickly.

"I'll eat breakfast with you," he said.

Corporal Trenholm walked over to stare out the window.

"I don't like it," he said. "You'll find that El Gato's gone on ahead. You're riding right into trouble."

Des thought of last night at the trough.

"El Gato's cleaner than he was, anyway," he said, hiding his concern. He told Corporal Trenholm about the ducking he'd given El Gato. And then, as the corporal laughed, about the first encounter at the stockyards.

"Three duckings and El Gato's out," Trenholm said, leading the way down the back stairs and out to the barn, throwing open the barn door and walking over the sill.

Des grinned and took a deep breath. It was hard to be frightened this morning, with the sun coming out, a slight gentle wind blowing off the Rockies, and Rocket turning his trusting brown eyes on Des. Yes, everything looked pretty rosy. He followed Corporal Trenholm across the sill and in beside Rocket.

"*Amigo,*" he whispered. "This is the day we make Lethbridge. Then, after one night's rest—the calf roping." He worked quickly, filling Rocket's manger with short buffalo-grass hay, and a gallon of crushed oats from a bin at the back of the barn. Then currying the sweat and straw from his big golden body, he saddled up.

In twenty minutes he sat opposite Corporal Trenholm.

"Bacon and eggs!" Des made a face as the girl in fresh red and white gingham put them before him. "What happens to all the beef?"

Trenholm smiled, slowly sipping his black coffee, then lapsed into thoughtful silence, eating with that steady purpose all western men get.

Des followed suit.

They hardly spoke till they'd settled their accounts, gone out to the barn and led their horses over to the water trough.

As the horses thrust their noses deep into the water, drinking noisily, Corporal Trenholm turned seriously to Des.

"Ride straight to Lethbridge," he ordered. "Put Rocket up at the Economy livery barn, directly behind the *King's Hotel.*"

Des nodded. It sounded simple.

Trenholm bridled his brown gelding and climbed into his saddle.

Des did likewise.

Their eyes met, and for a second, as he shifted his gaze to the flat prairie ahead, Des' stomach felt uneasy. What would El Gato do next?

"Wait till I come," Trenholm said, shortly. "I'll ride all night if I have to."

Des nodded, mustering a smile.

"Okay, Corporal," he said.

The two riders turned their horses by their reins, Trenholm to ride west toward the towering blue Porcupine Hills, and Des moving northeast across the flat monotonous grassland to strike the banks of the Old Man River, to follow it till the sun shifted from his face to his back. At length, when the sun cast a long shadow of Rocket and his rider on the grass, Des sighted Lethbridge across the river. Reining Rocket sharply to the right, he picked his way down to the water's edge. Holding his legs high above the swirling current, he put his horse across and up the other bank to the level prairie once more.

He paused.

Off to the left, Indian tepees thrust their cones into the dusk. Hordes of lean dogs milled before them and, just beyond, groups of hobbled Indian ponies grazed.

To the right stood the big grandstand, gay with the crossed flags of Canada and the United States, and the oval picket-fenced racecourse before it.

From the corrals opposite, came the bawl of calves.

Des caught his breath at the sound coming down the evening wind. His hand fell to his rope.

"*Amigo,*" he whispered into Rocket's upright ears, "Those are the guys that we rope tomorrow."

Rocket twitched his left ear, and Des, with a grin, touched him with his spurs and rode past the Indian camp and the stand toward a big brick building, dark against the skyline. That would be the *King's Hotel.*

At the edge of town Des took a back street till he came to the one leading up to the side of the hotel.

Rocket's ears were cocked. His body was wet with nervous sweat.

"Easy, *amigo,*" Des whispered, running his hand down the horse's lathered neck. "You've got to get used to city life, see?"

But Rocket didn't see.

As Des rode up to the corner by the hotel a streetcar clanged by.

Rocket reared, turned on his hind legs and with a terrified whinny broke for the prairie.

"Whoa, boy! Ouch!" Des pulled his reins, fighting a numb feeling in his right hand—his rope hand. "Must have struck my hand on the horn," he murmured.

After a quarter of a mile, Des got Rocket turned and edged him up toward the hotel once more.

There, dropping the reins, Des walked around the side of the brick building and with a sudden quick movement ducked through the door. El Gato was there—and a man with him. A big swarthy Mexican in a gaudy Mexican suit, on the curb, opposite.

Des forgot his dirty levis and grimy leather jumper. A sort of sickness came over him. Dumbly, he heard the slim young clerk at the desk say familiarly, "Sign here, Des Harmon—Corporal Trenholm phoned from Broken Arrow. Told us to watch out for you."

Des scrawled his name on the register, his mind racing.

"Want to go to your room?"

Des shook his head, wondering how he was going to get out and put Rocket in the Economy without El Gato's seeing him.

But in a moment he forgot even that—for a big kindly man with brown skin, nice eyes and a clipped moustache came up to the desk, and the clerk said heartily, "Yes, Señor Reyes, your room's ready. We got your wire from Dorado."

Des gulped and swung around. But it couldn't be—this man had on a business suit. A felt hat, all brown and civilized, no sombrero.

"Señor Reyes—Don Reyes who owns the *Sombrero Ranch*?" Des' lips formed the words in spite of him.

Señor Reyes met Des' eyes and laughed softly.

"You miss my sombrero—I am not dressed right?"

Des nodded, but suddenly snapped back to life.

El Gato still stood on the street corner, and the dark

Mexican in the tight pants and beaded jacket was with him. One of these men was a fake.

He said, then, "I am Des Harmon——" And watching Señor Reyes' face he knew that the name meant nothing to him.

Des tried again.

"I have just come in with a wild horse I caught on Soda Springs range—a Palomino?"

"A Palomino, then he is the good horse. The best horse in the world for roping," Señor Reyes said, innocently. He moved closer, fingering Des' lariat. "You are a roper, perhaps? You are going to compete tomorrow?"

Des knew then, that if this man was Señor Reyes he certainly hadn't received his letter. Des nodded.

"Yes, I am going to try for the calf roping."

"Good, I will be there to watch," Reyes said, gently.

The clerk snickered.

"I am to be a judge," Reyes explained.

Des gulped again, and for a moment felt the icy fear of tomorrow's contest grip him. Suddenly, he shrugged it off, and broke for the front door. Then, remembering El Gato, turned back to the clerk.

"Is there a side door—I left my horse out there?"

"Beyond the stairs," the clerk pointed.

Des found the side door and walked through it and out to Rocket—and El Gato, with his fat friend.

"Hello, *amigo*," El Gato said, a slow triumphant grin spreading over his swarthy face. He gestured easily to the man beside him. "This is Señor Don Reyes of Dorado. He will take the horse—tell you how he belongs to me."

"*Si, si!*" The fat Mexican's disks jangled on his short buckskin jacket as he jerked his arms. "Thees colt we vent on the banks of the Rio de Sonora. But before we burn El Gato's box brand on, he is kick off the ropes! He is gone!"

Des didn't know for sure which man was the real Don Reyes but he took a chance.

"Rocket, here, was just a yearling then?" He asked. "He should remember you?"

"*Si, si!*" The Mexican nodded, grinning. "He was one smart colt—that I loved."

Des got an inkling of Rocket's feelings—his ears flattened, his eyes fixed brightly on the fat, gesticulating Mexican.

"Then you think he loves you—that you can lead him away like a dog?" Des said, his heart beating fast. For what if the man could—and did? What if he took the reins and led Rocket away forever?

"*Si, si*—like a dog!" The fat Mexican's face broke into a wider grin. He shot a look of triumph at El Gato, shrugging.

"Good!" Like a shot, Des handed Rocket's reins to the Mexican. "Here he is!"

Des could scarcely breathe. He heard a window in the hotel raise with a squawk, the sound of a whistle in the distance. What if Rocket went with the Mexican?

Suddenly the air seemed full of Rocket's pounding hoofs. He reared above the screaming Mexican, who stumbled, put up his hands, crawled on all fours out of Rocket's way, then with El Gato after him, ran toward the street.

Des quieted Rocket, taking his reins and patting his sweaty neck.

"I guess," he said, sadly, "that we've found the real Don Reyes."

"*Si*," a voice behind him said.

Des wiped a hand across his tired eyes.

"I guess, too, *amigo*, that we've found the man who owns you."

Turning to Don Reyes, he pulled back Rocket's mane.

"The sombrero," he said, and handed Rocket's reins to Señor Reyes. "It's your brand and your horse."

For a moment, Des wildly hoped that Rocket would disown Don Reyes. But staring, with a lump in his throat, he saw the horse hesitate, then, seeming to bring back something from a long way, put his nose against Don Reyes' ear and nibble, gently.

Des gulped.

"*Amigo.*" It was Reyes' voice, and it had a tremble in it. "I am sorry I sold you."

Des jumped. His eyes searched the kindly glowing ones of Don Reyes. "S-sold him—then you do not own Rocket?"

Don Reyes' hand went to the sombrero brand, then on to the bar beneath.

"The vent," he said, simply.

Des' heart hit his boot tops.

"Then, El Gato does own him?" He took Rocket's mane to steady himself, his eyes still on Don Reyes.

"Not El Gato, but another—an American."

Des' lips formed the word, "Who?" He could see Rocket slipping farther away than ever.

Don Reyes shook his head.

"That," he said, picking his words, "I can only tell you tomorrow. It is why I am here. Tomorrow, if I find out the owner of this horse is here—and alive, he will take him. Otherwise"—he shrugged—"I will take him back to Mexico to hold in trust."

"But if the man is dead? If I win the calf roping and pay you the money for Rocket to hold in trust?" Des asked, his heart thudding so he could hardly talk.

"Let us wait and see," Don Reyes said, moving off into the gloom.

Des picked up Rocket's reins and led him toward the Economy, using his left hand, for the right was swollen around the thumb. The thumb he'd have to use to win the calf roping; maybe, to buy a horse from its owner, or Don Reyes, maybe?

He walked on, his thumb throbbing, his heart filled with a big question. But one thing, he knew, he had to win the calf roping, thumb or no thumb.

CHAPTER XII

THE ROPING CONTEST

DES AWOKE AS THE FIRST STREAKS OF LIGHT SLASHED THE cloudless eastern sky. Getting out of bed and favoring his right thumb, that "crunched" when he wiggled it, Des dressed gingerly.

"Not so good, thumb," he said softly, splashing water on his face and wetting down his dark hair. "But good or not"—he grinned wryly down at it—"you're the one I've got to win that calf roping with today."

Quietly he let himself out of the room, down the hall and stairs, then out the big front door. No El Gato lounging on the curb—that cookie was washed up. But, as he walked around the end of the *King's Hotel* and along the back street to the Economy, Des felt his heart squeeze shut. He almost wished El Gato did own Rocket. At least he was here, to be seen, maybe dickered with. He wasn't some mystery guy who might not show up at all—sending Rocket back to Mexico with Don Reyes.

Des walked through the barn door. Rocket nickered from his stall and began to prance impatiently.

A big lump in his throat, Des walked in beside him.

122

He couldn't breathe for the pain of thinking this might be the last time he'd saddle that big golden body.

"*Amigo,*" he whispered, rustling crushed oats and hay for the manger. "You've got to be good today—right on the calf, see?"

Rocket seemed to savvy. He stood quietly munching his oats as Des carefully saddled up, giving particular care to the condition of Rocket's back, seeing that no dust lay between the blanket and the saddle.

At last the big sleek horse stood ready for the contest ahead.

"Okay, *amigo,*" Des whispered, slapping Rocket's big thigh. "Eat hearty, you'll need it." Turning from the stall, he walked back to the main street and down it half a block to the *Hot Iron Cafe.*

"Eggs and bacon," he ordered, smiling sheepishly into the mirror in front of him.

"Gets to be a habit, pardner?" A voice beside him drawled. "Like partin' your hair."

Des turned and after a quick glance all but fell off his stool.

"Jim Fleet!" he exclaimed. Everybody knew Jim Fleet's tall gangly frame, his steel-blue eyes, that hint of a smile at the corners of a wide generous mouth. Des' heart began to hammer. He wished he hadn't run into him. Jim's time in the calf roping was twenty-one and two-fifths seconds—half a second behind El Gato's, but—

Jim grinned, studying Des' ever-present rope dangling from his arm.

"Let's see," he said, suddenly forgetting to eat the stack of hot cakes before him, and taking the rope from Des. "Boy!" He took both hands to the rope—big raw-boned hands that handled the braided lariat with the deftness of a violinist with his bow. He turned to Des.

"It's kind of a funny thing to ask," he drawled. "But my rope's gone sour on me—if I could use this one, today?"

Des reddened to the roots of his sunburned hair. Wildly he stared around, trying to think of some excuse — Finally, he brought his eyes back to Jim's.

"I'd sure like to—except that I'm using it myself."

Jim Fleet's eyes took in Des Harmon for the first time. Suddenly, they crinkled at the corners. "Sure enough—the kid Corporal Trenholm phoned in the last-minute entry for."

Des' jaw dropped. He'd intended doing that after breakfast. "Trenholm tended to it yesterday?"

Fleet nodded.

What happened after that wasn't quite clear to Des. He heard a lot of laughter from others lined up at the counter, and felt his rope slide back on his wiry arm.

And out on the sidewalk, he felt his neck. It had a big new silk bandanna around it—Jim Fleet's. And his words still sang in Des' ears. "Kid, here's something to give you luck." He'd been looking down at Des' swollen thumb.

Big Jim Fleet was a cinch to take the roping and the five-hundred-dollar prize. Even El Gato—well named The Cat, being so nimble with his hands—feared him. His voice from down the counter had sounded boasting, and as if trying to hide his fear, as he said, "Today, I hang up new record—maybe nineteen and two-fifths seconds, to tie the calf."

Walking back to Rocket, Des knew that the one thing he had to do was win. Win, or bust.

Bridling Rocket and leading him out of the barn, Des rode west till he came to the river. Dropping down the banks to the stream, he waded the horse out in it, waiting impatiently as Rocket drank.

A herd of cows and calves trailed slowly down to the water. Des pulled Rocket's reins and rode toward them, uncoiling his rope, making a small loop—one that a calf wouldn't jump through before he could jerk it shut.

A calf broke from its mother and skirted the riverbank.

"Okay, amigo." Des put the great gold stallion after him.

It was a short race. The calf, frantic and bawling, was no match for Rocket's piston-like legs. In seconds, he was right on that flying ball of red fuzz.

Des, counting in what he thought was seconds, leaned out over his saddle and sent his rope singing through the air. A sharp pain shot through his thumb just as the rope left his hand. And he'd missed—the rope sailing off to the right, the calf scampering on to freedom.

It didn't matter that Des put Rocket in pursuit and, on the next throw, still counting the seconds, tied the calf in twenty-one and two-fifths seconds. One miss like that and the contest was lost.

"No ketchum prize that way," a faraway voice mourned, as Des loosed the calf and let it run bawling to its anxious mother.

Des jerked upright. His eyes went over the silent moody Indian boy sitting his pinto horse.

"White Cloud—what you doing here?"

"Watch you," White Cloud grunted. "You big chump think can win calf roping."

Des had that all figured out.

"Lynn come?" He asked. He could use a sight of that friendly face in the crowd this afternoon.

"Nope—send me," White Cloud said. His black eyes looked stolidly on Des as they might on a horse who'd eaten locoweed. "You know El Gato tie calf in twenty and two-fifths seconds—Jim Fleet plenty fast, too?"

Des nodded. He jumped clear off the deep end.

"I will tie calf today in nineteen seconds flat," he heard his voice say.

White Cloud shook his head. He was still shaking it as he rode with Des, out the graded road to the fair grounds through the contestants' gate and over to the big whitewashed plank corrals and bucking chutes.

The bucking-horse contest was on, now.

A white and pink horse rolled from the open chute bawling, trying to throw the puncher, who wore scarlet shirt and white chaps.

"From chute one—Rodgers on Pink Tea!" droned the announcer.

Des hoped Jim wouldn't be there right then. But he was.

"Howdy," he said, walking up. "How's the thumb, cowboy?"

Des managed a grin and moved it around. "Okay," he said.

He looked across the contest ground to the grandstand packed with people. They spilled out on the space in front. Indians wrapped in red-and-white striped Hudson's Bay blankets paraded around—their faces bright with paint; eagle feathers stuck in their jet-black hair.

Des' heart sank. There were Don Reyes and Jim Starr

and Nina. Des gripped his saddle horn to stay on. Then Rocket's owner hadn't shown up? For a second, Des thought of giving up. What was the use of winning the calf-roping money if it wouldn't buy Rocket. But staring at Reyes and Jim and Nina laughing and talking up there in the tenth row of the stands, Des knew that he couldn't quit. Something within him wouldn't let him quit.

He saw the pickup riders go out to lift Rodgers from Pink Tea. Heard the splash of applause for his ride.

For what seemed hours it went on.

Des couldn't think. Only that dumbness crept through him. His hand hurt.

"Bailey on Sudden Death! Sparks on Bean Shooter!" the loud-speaker system ground on. And finally with, "Rodgers wins the Bucking-horse Contest!" sputtered a moment, then blared, "Next event, the Cowboy Race —followed by the Pony Race. And then, the Calf Roping."

"That's us," Fleet said, climbing into his saddle. "First three winners in the Cowboy Race compete in the Calf Roping." He put spurs to his roan and danced out in front of the grandstand to the starting line.

"Yipee—Fleet!" roared the stands. Everybody knew Jim Fleet and Diamond, his roan rope horse.

"El Gato! The champion!" came next. A hush followed his entrance, then a buzz of excited talk.

Going over his record, Des grimly knew. He put Rocket's big golden head toward the half-dozen contestants and rode out on the track.

"Rocket!" a lone voice called. "Go to it, Rocket!"

That was Nina Starr, Des knew. His throat went dry. At least one person in the stands wanted him to win.

"Line up," the judges ordered.

The horses, prancing, their necks foamy under their manes, minced to the starting line.

Des kept Rocket's head pointed straight down the track.

"Easy, *amigo*," he whispered, straining his ears to catch the crack of the starting pistol.

Then suddenly it did explode.

A shout rose from the stands.

Des loosed Rocket's reins, giving him his head. The great horse, his powerful legs moving rhythmically, sped down the track, pulled away from the roan, from El Gato's black.

A gasp of sheer wonder burst from the stands.

"Rocket!" came from a thousand throats.

Des, his heart singing, rode him lightly, to the half mile, to the three-quarters, to where the finish tape loomed ahead, to where it looked as though Rocket couldn't lose.

Suddenly, the big horse swerved, turned in spite of all Des could do, and with the range instinct, rounded behind the horses sweeping to the finish line, and herded them across it—coming in last.

Des reddened, pulling Rocket to a halt. He heard the guffaws of laughter sweeping the stands and the loud-speaker blare, "El Gato on La Culebra wins. Fleet on Diamond, second; Rodgers on Midnight, third. Next event, the Indian Pony Race—followed by the Calf Roping for the championship of Western Canada."

Des rode Rocket slowly back to the corrals.

The bawl of calves filled his ears with an ache. His eyes stung with the alkali dust rising from their pound-ing hoofs in the pens, as the punchers cut the roping calves into the "ready" chutes. This was the end. He'd lost the right to compete for the five hundred. Lost Rocket, for good, too.

El Gato rode by, sneering, "You lose horse, *si*?"

The loud-speaker confirmed it, after the hubbub of the Indian Pony Race: "Competing for the Calf-roping Championship by right of winning the Cowboy Race, "El Gato on La Culebra, Jim Fleet on Diamond, and Roy Rodgers on Midnight," it blared.

Des got off Rocket and eased his cinch with aching

hands. But suddenly his head spun around. What was that the stands shouted?

"The kid on Rocket! The kid on Rocket! Rocket! Rocket!"

The shouts went on and on, with Des wishing they would stop. He was a good sport. He could take losing —wasn't asking any special favors.

But it seemed he was to have no choice in the matter.

The loud-speaker crackled. The crowd hushed. And in the silence, dropping like a rock inside Des' head, plumbed the words, "By special request, an added contestant in the Calf Roping, Des Harmon on Rocket!"

The crowd went crazy. Yelling and shouting and laughing. Men slapping each other on the back—women laughing and nodding to one another.

And out by the corrals, Des gulped. He felt the sweat roll down along his back as he drew for position: First try, Rodgers, then Fleet, El Gato, and last of the four— himself. They were to have one calf each and three tries.

"*Si.*" El Gato smiled and winked at Des. "But one calf missed—poof! The contest she is lost!" His beady black eyes bored into Des'.

Des turned away and walked back to Rocket. His hands could scarcely move as he loosened the saddle, moved it well forward on Rocket's back, then cinched it tight.

"Can't have it slip, *amigo*," he breathed, softly.

Rocket's soft nose came down along Des' cheek.

It made a lump come into Des' throat, and a column of steel run along his back. It eased that pain inside him, and let him laugh at Rodgers' first calf, a little speckled thing that leaped from the chute and never gave Rodgers a chance to overtake it.

"Rodgers out—no catch," said the merciless loud-speaker.

Des gulped, and saw that Don Reyes had left the stands to take his place in the judges' booth—a little round raised house well out from the stands.

Fleet lined up, giving the gateman the nod.

His calf came—a black with a slow deceptive run.

Fleet overthrew, took a second shot and downed him.

"Fleet's time: twenty-nine and four-fifths seconds."

"Good for a second throw, that time," Rodgers said. "But second throws won't win here."

"*Si!*" El Gato said. He touched his black lightly, as his calf, a rangy brindle, fled past the line. With a swirl of black on brown, he tossed his calf flat, leaped from his horse and tied the calf with a flourish, raising his hands in the air.

"Time, El Gato—twenty-three seconds, flat."

"Tie that," taunted El Gato, riding by Des.

Des barely nodded, his eyes on chute four. They saw

a red calf leap from it, then reach and pass the penalty line.

The whistle—for the roper to start.

Des put Rocket after the fleeing calf, leaning low, swinging his rope in short quick circles around his head.

The calf was fifteen feet ahead. Ten feet.

Des leaned over Rocket's ears and sent his rope, a live thing, out and down— He'd missed—no! He felt the rope sing taut on the saddle horn.

With a leap, he jumped down, followed the rope to the wriggling bawling calf. Two quick flips with his hands under the calf's foreleg and flank, a wind of his tie rope around its hind legs and one front one, and Des sprang erect, throwing his hands into the air.

"The kid—twenty-three seconds, flat," blared the loud-speaker.

"El Gato's time!" Des' heart bumped his ribs. He loosed his calf, coiled his rope and gently rode past the hazers, running the calf back into the chutes. *"Amigo,"* he whispered to Rocket, "we are holding our own."

Rocket shook his head and blew out his breath.

The second round of calves started.

A shout that gave place to a groan rose from the stands as Jim Fleet missed his second calf, couldn't get his rope coiled in time. and watched its black body skip over the finish line.

"No catch—Fleet out," droned the announcer.

"It is you and me, eh, kid?" El Gato smirked, spring-ing lightly into his low flat Mexican saddle.

Des nodded, "Yes, you and me." The gate creaked open to let El Gato's second calf ooze through it.

"El Gato's time, second calf, twenty-one and two-fifths seconds," the announcer said, almost instantly. He said it as though he dared Des to equal it.

Des heard it through a fog. What was the use of trying any further? A panic struck him, feeling the big horse under him—the horse that would go back to Mexico prize money or no prize money.

But Rocket wouldn't let Des quit. The big stallion seemed to enter the game. He fairly smothered Des' second calf, a lean red bull, a moment after he catapulted from the chute and made it across the penalty line. In half a hundred leaping bounds, Rocket was on him, following his every corkscrew turn, till Des had only to reach down and drop the loop over that bullet head, then slip off and make the tie.

"Time, the kid, second calf: twenty-one and two-fifths seconds."

"No! It's crazy! Crazy!" roared the stands. "Time-keeper's crazy—two alike." It had never happened. But it had.

Des made it back to the corrals, his knees like water.

"Kid, you've tied the world's record." Fleet grinned, lifting him to the dusty ground. "And with a bum thumb."

"But not a new one—watch. I tie my third calf in nineteen and two-fifths," El Gato boasted, piling into his saddle, his lithe brown hands coiling his rope for the final catch.

And he did just that, with the crowd going wild, and the white calf loping away after El Gato released him.

"El Gato's final calf," the announcer crowed. "Nineteen and two-fifths seconds—a new world's record."

Through the thunderous applause, El Gato sneered to Des, "*Gracias*, I can use that five hundred."

Des climbed into his saddle. His thumb hurt. Icy sweat ran down his back. He had a kink in his rope. And the calf, the color of dry grass, was leaping from the chute. It was over the line! And he hadn't even started!

But Rocket had. The great golden horse reared and plunged for the calf. In less than fifty long fleeing leaps he was over it.

Des, his rope circling, leaned for the throw.

The calf dodged, turned back and—*under* Rocket's legs.

Des heard the stands gasp.

This was it. This was the end, knifed through his

mind. It seemed as though life slowed for him, and he knew he felt Rocket's body under him for the last time.

Only force of habit, and the fighting instinct of a guy who wouldn't quit, made him lean low in his saddle, see the grass-colored calf come out the other side of Rocket, swing across and fling the loop.

He had the calf.

But the animal had dodged back under Rocket's belly. The rope was beginning to tighten. A warning, as from a bell rang in Des' head: "Rocket'll go crazy if that rope tightens and touches his belly!"

With a cry, Des leaped from the saddle and on the calf. He downed him before the rope pulled taut, flung him to the ground, and with his lariat tangled in his legs and those of the calf, made the tie. Up shot his hands into the air.

For what seemed an age, not a sound came from the breathless stands.

The loud-speaker, for once, seemed dumb.

Rocket's blowing came soft and free—the breathing of a horse with power in reserve.

Des felt ice form around his heart.

And then, above the crack of a bronc's hoof on a corral plank, the announcer's voice welled out, "Ladies and gentlemen, a new world's record—nineteen and one-fifth seconds for Des Harmon. He wins the Calf-roping Championship of the world."

Des heard the shouts from the stands as though in a daze. All he could see was Don Reyes coming slowly across the field—and Jim Starr and Nina.

Des released his calf, then turned to throw an arm around Rocket's sweaty neck.

"So long, *amigo*," he whispered, then turned to face Don Reyes.

"Oh, Des"— Nina's freckled face seemed alive with excitement—"you won! The calf roping, *amigo*, everything!"

Des stared. But of course she didn't understand. He met Don Reyes' eyes.

"Well, sir," he said, squaring his shoulders. "I see the owner didn't show up—here's your horse." He tried to hand Rocket's reins to Don Reyes.

"Oh, the owner didn't show up, eh?" Jim Starr stepped forward to take the reins.

Des looked from Jim's face to Nina's, then on to Don Reyes'. But Jim Starr's chuckle brought his eyes back to him.

"You, Rocket's owner?" Des faltered. His mind raced back to the morning on the river, when Rocket had seemed to know Jim Starr.

Jim grinned.

"Yep," he said. "And after what you did for me, who do you think owns him now?"

Nina's peal of laughter at Des' red face, and Reyes nodding rapidly and saying, *"Si, Si,"* told Des the truth. He protested. He said flatly, "He's your horse, Mr. Starr —just because you didn't get time to brand him that day down on the Rio de Sonora—" But all the time Jim was pressing the reins in his hands, and Rocket's big soft nose slid along his cheek.

Suddenly, Des' knees got weak.

"Mine, all mine," he whispered.

"Sure, all yours—and now you'd better go and collect your money."

Jim Starr lifted Des into the saddle and Des, with a flourish, rode over to the judges' stand.

"The kid! Rocket! The Palomino!" cheered the rapidly emptying stands.

Des rode up to the stand. He gently pressed Rocket's reins and the big horse reared high on his hindlegs, then dropped to the ground and stood quiet.

The judge, George Roark, Jim Fleet's boss, stepped down and handed Des five one-hundred-dollar bills.

"Nice work, Des," he said.

Des pocketed the money, whispering, "Thank you,"

and Rocket dipped his head letting his silver foretop drop deep over his brown eyes. Des could have died for pride in him.

"Rocket! The Palomino!" came a final cheer, with spattering applause.

Des lifted Rocket's head with a touch of the reins. gave him spur, and raced toward Nina and Jim and Don Reyes.

But midfield, a black horse blocked him. And as the two horses collided, El Gato leaned over and said, with the softness of a cat, "It is still many miles to the *Twin Anchor, si*—?"

Des opened his mouth to reply. But before he could speak, El Gato had gone. Des slowly gathered Rocket's reins and rode toward Nina and Jim. If he were only home. If he didn't have that thirty-eight miles of flat. prairie to cover. There, more than one had an advantage —there, men on horses could sweep from both sides, cutting their quarry off.

Suddenly, Des leaned down and ran a hand along Rocket's powerful neck.

"Rocket," he whispered, coming close to the group, and sensing that what he said was true. "Tomorrow, you will prove yourself—if we are to make *Twin Anchor* at all."

CHAPTER XIII

CHASE FOR HOME

NEXT MORNING DES WOKE TO THE SOUND OF A LASHING rain on the window pane of his hotel bedroom. *Twin Anchor Ranch* seemed far across a wet world from the dripping *King's Hotel*.

When Des fought through the storm to the Economy, Rocket made it look still farther away. His right front foot was off the plank floor, and he kept nosing it with tender care.

Des moodily examined it, then came back to stand staring through the doorway into the dripping half light of dawn. Uncertainly, he shifted from one booted foot to the other. Corporal Trenholm hadn't come—hadn't showed up at all. If he were only here, Des mused, he'd know what to do. Probably, though, he'd been held up at Broken Arrow.

But suddenly, Des knew, too.

He walked back into the stall and picked up Rocket's foot. Running a deft hand down the leg, Des sized the situation up—no puffiness. Just a slight strain.

"Probably smooth out in half an hour—and we're on our way," he decided.

Des groomed the Palomino, saddled him, taking special care with his bedroll, and the things he'd bought for Janet and his mother and Harry.

"A doll for Janet, so she won't have to dress that pup. A dress for Mom"—he wanted to see her eyes when she put it on— "And a new rope for Harry." He'd been a plenty-good guy to stay home.

Des finished tying the bedroll on behind his saddle, then, while Rocket snorted and kicked, and bunted the hay around his manger, sat down and munched the cheese and crackers he'd rustled for this early getaway.

It was still an hour till daylight. And he'd not take any chances. He'd slip along the river, then angle south and hit the flat straight road to the *Twin Anchor*.

Des took a big bite of crackers and cheese, and grinned. If El Gato thought he knew a thing or two about trailing, well, he had a few ideas himself.

At length, with the murky light of a wet dawn outlining the buildings of Lethbridge, Des led Rocket out, let him drink at the trough just inside the door, bridled him, then climbed into the saddle.

A lump in his levis money pocket, just under the tooled leather belt he'd bought himself, warmed Des.

"Boy, that four hundred and fifty'll buy plenty of groceries till Dad gets home."

He put the spurs to Rocket and rode out into the

pouring rain. The spatter of water on his new Stetson made Des grin ruefully. But he shrugged, turning Rocket toward the river. If a hat wouldn't stand this, it was a good time to find it out.

He made it to the edge of the riverbanks. Off to the left, the Indian tepees looked like smudged upside-down ice-cream cones.

A dog barked as Des rode past. Three others took it up. Then a dozen. Bedlam broke loose.

Rocket reared and plunged.

Des fought to quiet him, wondering why Rocket seemed so nervous.

Suddenly, at the last tepee before dipping down to the river, a sleepy head came through the tent flap. Two big black eyes stared stolidly at Des. It was White Cloud, again.

"Ketchum *Twin Anchor*," he grunted. "You plenty smart go in rain—fool El Gato."

Des, with a wave of his hand, rode on. But for the first time, a slight premonition of failure filled him.

"Wish that guy'd been sure I wouldn't make it," he groused to Rocket. "I'd feel surer of turning the trick."

A special gust of wind dashed rain down his neck. He slid Rocket down along the river and picked his way south and a little east.

A clump of chokecherry bushes ahead rustled.

Des stared in the half light of coming day, quieted Rocket, who was having a fit.

"Was that a head? And the rump of a black horse?"

Des put Rocket at the bushes and rode slowly around them. At length, he grinned sheepishly.

"Seein' things," he whispered, in disgust.

Rocket nodded his head, and rolled his big spade bit in his teeth. Ever since he'd left the barn, he'd been jumpy; scenting an inevitable race, through Des, and wanting to get going.

They rode on downriver five miles, then turned up to the road. Des, looking around the horizon, grinned.

The rain had slackened. As far as the eye could see there was only prairie. Rain clouds hovered over, but through them the sunshine came out. The wind swung to the west and suddenly the ground was dry underfoot.

Just a local shower—we've ridden out of it, Des thought. His eyes went ahead to the blue Milk River Ridge. Home—just at the foot of those hills. He looked around the horizon once again. Not a rider in sight. No closing in from both sides as he'd feared.

And yet, Rocket pranced and fought his bit. A light sweat broke out all over him, and his eyes, usually so steady, rolled and grew bloodshot.

Des pulled him to a walk.

"Take it easy." he said, confidently. "We're okay."

His words died on his lips as, off to the left and ahead, loomed the magnified size of a rider!

Des gasped, and looked to the right. Another rider! Well ahead, too. Cunningly ahead, as was the first. They'd ride together, squeezing him. It was suddenly plain to Des. They were riding funnelwise. Ahead, maybe ten miles, lay Pot Hole—a long coulee through which he'd have to ride. And they were going to squeeze him in it.

Too late to back out, now.

And anyway—a stubborn streak came out in Des—he'd licked El Gato all the way, so far. Why couldn't he do it again?

Gently, he put Rocket's pace faster. The horse's foot had smoothed out; he was really stretching out.

The riders increased their speed.

Des knew that he had but one chance—to outrun those men to Pot Hole. Taking a deep breath, he shoved the spurs gently into Rocket's steaming ribs.

"You've been wanting this race," he said, grimly. "Now, here it is."

The great horse bounded forward.

Simultaneously, the two riders on the sides spurred forward.

A mile, two miles, Rocket sped on.

The riders, well in the lead, began to close in.

Des' heart bumped his ribs. He leaned low in his saddle.

Another mile sped by.

Now, Des could make out the riders.

"James," he whispered, taking in the long lank form of the rider to his right. "One of the Robber's Roost gang."

He put the spurs to Rocket in earnest then.

The thud of his hoofs rang out on the prairie.

They all raced for the head of Pot Hole Coulee, its chalky cliffs lying dead ahead.

Des bent down along Rocket's mane. He could hear the flying horse's steady breathing and knew they'd make it. But the rider to the left turned straight in, gambling all on his swift horse.

"The Mexican," Des breathed, letting Rocket have his head. "The bogus Reyes."

Rocket swept down the trail, head up, silver tail streaming out behind.

A half mile—a quarter—separated the three straining horses. Then, suddenly, with a last mighty surging effort, Rocket squeezed between the closing riders and carried Des into the lead.

Bullets whistled overhead. One chipped a rock to the right of Rocket then ricocheted into the air, its horrid whine sounding above the Mexican's fading curse.

Des sped on. He was free of them—free. And putting more distance between himself and his pursuers.

Down the Pot Hole Des swept, and along its two miles to a bridge. Then around a sharp bend—and there, sitting his black horse, a blunt-nosed gun in his hand, smiled El Gato.

Des checked Rocket, his great black hoofs plowing deep in the gravel.

Behind, came the distant thud of his pursuers. On either side rose the banks of Pot Hole Coulee. Only one way out—straight ahead. Straight through El Gato.

Des caught his breath, tightened his hold on Rocket's reins, and with a soft whisper put the big golden stallion straight at the waiting Mexican.

El Gato leveled his revolver.

"Alto!" he commanded.

Des shut his ears and lay almost flat against the charging horse. The lathered foam spattered his drawn face. The smell of sweat stung his eyes, fixed on El Gato's gun.

It spat.

Des felt his hat jump and knew a moment's anger. His new Stetson drilled.

But the gun spoke no more. It wavered in the unnerved El Gato's hands, as he screamed in terror of the vengeful Rocket.

The golden horse, ears back, eyes gleaming, closed the distance between him and the black—twenty-five feet, twenty, ten—

El Gato wildly flung the gun away trying to swerve his horse. But too late.

The big stallion hit the two broadside.

Des clung, against the impact. He saw the big black lurch, then go down, carrying the screaming El Gato beneath. Des knew then that El Gato would always fear Rocket—never again try to get him. His heart leaped. For now El Gato was through, and they were free! But instantly, he knew that they were not. The blow against the black had been too much for Rocket. He faltered, stumbled the length of himself, tried vainly to keep his feet, then catapulted into a golden heap on the grass.

Des sailed over his head and, hitting the ground with a thud, lay still. The dull pound of distant hoofs filled his numb ears as he lay. It seemed to be drawing closer.

Des could only lie staring up at the scudding clouds while a giant hand seemed holding him down.

The pounding hoofs came closer. A shout rang out.

Des wondered who was yelling?

Suddenly, a soft nose thrust into his face. A cascade of silver hair tickled it, getting into his eyes. He closed them. Boy, he was tired—tired! And he wished that pounding would quit.

The nose jostled him again. Then a hoof pawed at his shoulder. Des opened his eyes.

"Rocket," he whispered. "Rocket, ol' boy."

The pounding filled his ears.

Des raised on an elbow to see where it came from. He saw El Gato stretched on the ground, his left leg off at a funny angle, and his black standing over him.

"El Gato!" With a rush, Des came back to earth. "And James and the Mexican—they weren't fifty yards distant!"

Des tried to stand. His legs wouldn't hold him. He sank down to the grass.

Rocket shook his great head, moving in close to Des.

Des tried again. He pulled himself by the stirrups—into the saddle. And hung to the horn—

The big horse swung, and with Des' world going in a drunken dizzy circle, set his piston-like legs going in that long ground-eating pace.

But too late. Des knew it was too late.

The two riders sandwiched him between them. They closed less than fifty feet away.

"He's ours!" James yelled. His rope sang through the air.

But Rocket ducked the loop, then doubled between them. He ran a hundred feet before the two men could turn their horses, then with Des lurching in the saddle, skirted in a wide arc and fled. His blinding speed, once he got going, carried Des to safety, and on toward *Twin Anchor*— Looking back, Des knew that James and the Mexican would look after El Gato.

It was pitch-dark when Des cut off from the highway and up the trail to the *Twin Anchor*.

Riding into the yard, he had a feeling of neglect and lonesomeness. His head ached from his tumble, and hunger gnawed at his flat stomach.

"No one in sight," Des groused. "Just a light in the kitchen window. Not even the pup to bark at me."

Des rode up to the kitchen door, then suddenly wheeled Rocket toward the barn.

"Well, if that was all anybody cared?"

Suddenly the kitchen door opened and light flooded into the yard.

"Des! It's Des! O-oh! An' on the biggest gold horse in the wo—rrrld!" shrieked Janet.

"Look out," Des warned, gruffly. He slipped to the ground and just had time to wipe his eyes on Rocket's mane before a deep voice said, "Des—!"

Des looked up at that.

"Dad!" he exclaimed. "A furlough?"

Dad in blue uniform, nodded slowly. "Maybe a long one—the way the war's going. Boy!" He whistled. "Look, Mom—what Des brought home."

"Boy, is right!" Harry breathed, reverently taking Rocket's reins.

All at once, Des was tongued-tied. Words stuck in his throat. But he managed to blurt out, "He's yours, for the herd, Dad. From Harry and me. A purebred Palomino from Don Reyes' ranch on the Rio de Sonora."

"Wonderful, boys," Dad said. "A new sire for the *Twin Anchor.*" Suddenly, there in the dark, he faced Des and Harry. "Do you realize that you've saved the ranch—that we can pay Hawkins off. Everything we owe him, when the foals begin to come."

"An' Hawkins can go jump in the lake, an' his bank, too," piped Janet.

"Child!" Mrs. Harmon chided.

Dad grinned, scooping Janet into his arms. Des looked at Harry, then dived for his pants' pocket.

"Before that, Dad—" he said, softly, pulling out the roll of money. "I won a calf-roping contest up in Lethbridge. There's four hundred and fifty dollars here to pay Hawkins."

Dad took the money, blinking hard. And Harry caught his breath, then suddenly woke up with a whoop.

"You won the calf-roping! Honest?"

Des, coloring, ducked to untie his bedroll and rummage for his mother's dress, Janet's doll and Harry's rope. "Aw, it was nothing," he protested.

Janet wriggled out of her father's arms and came over to stare up at Des with unwinking eyes.

"He wins the World's Championship Calf-Roping title and it's nothing!" She waved a skinny brown arm to the soft night breeze.

Everybody laughed.

Des found the presents and began giving them out. His hands shook. But inside, he felt his heart swell. He was home, and he'd brought Rocket.